“For the sake of Marley, we will both be sleeping in this bed.”

Tara quirked a brow. “For her sake?”

“She still has nightmares,” Sam told her. “If she crawls into bed and I’m sleeping on the floor or on the sofa, do you want to answer all those questions? This will get better,” he assured her as he pulled his shirt over his head. “I’m confident her memories will...”

Sam lost all train of thought at the sight of Tara staring at his exposed chest.

“This won’t work,” she muttered. “I mean, I’m still attracted to you, but I don’t want to be.”

* * *

RETURN TO STONEROCK:
In this small Tennessee town,
neighbors find the warmth of home...and love

Dear Reader,

The wait is over! Sam and Tara are here, along with their sweet daughter, Marley. I wanted to do a spin on the traditional amnesia story, so I hope you love this journey.

If you read *The Cowboy's Second-Chance Family* and *From Best Friend to Daddy*, then you have already met Sam and Tara. This dynamic couple has truly been through so much and they are finally going to get their happy ending…after jumping a few more hurdles, of course.

Sam is one determined man and he wants his family back. I don't believe I've ever written a stronger hero, and Tara…well, she's afraid of getting hurt again. She might be a little hard on Sam, but that all stems from past pain.

I hope this book touches you as much as it did me. Addiction is a very serious topic and one I feel has touched nearly every family in one way or another.

In this final installment of my Return to Stonerock series, I promise all the feels and a few "aww" moments as Sam and Tara learn to love again and rebuild their marriage stronger than ever.

Happy reading,

Jules

For Their Child's Sake

Jules Bennett

Recycling programs for this product may not exist in your area.

ISBN-13: 978-1-335-57393-3

For Their Child's Sake

This edition published by arrangement with Harlequin Books S.A.

For questions and comments about the quality of this book, please contact us at CustomerService@Harlequin.com.

Printed in U.S.A.

USA TODAY bestselling author **Jules Bennett** has published over sixty books and never tires of writing happy endings. Creating strong heroines and alpha heroes is Jules's favorite way to spend her workdays. Jules hosts weekly contests on her Facebook fan page and loves chatting with readers on Twitter, Facebook and via email through her website. Stay up-to-date by signing up for her newsletter at julesbennett.com.

Books by Jules Bennett

Harlequin Special Edition

Return to Stonerock

The Cowboy's Second-Chance Family

The St. Johns of Stonerock

Dr. Daddy's Perfect Christmas
The Fireman's Ready-Made Family
From Best Friend to Bride

Harlequin Desire

What the Prince Wants
A Royal Amnesia Scandal
Maid for a Magnate
His Secret Baby Bombshell
Best Man Under the Mistletoe
Married in Name Only

The Rancher's Heirs

Twin Secrets
Claimed by the Rancher

Visit her Author Profile page at Harlequin.com, or julesbennett.com, for more titles.

To anyone who has struggled with addiction of any kind, there is hope. You are not forgotten.

Chapter One

"Just tell us the prognosis."

Sam Bailey had been on an emotional roller coaster the past two years. And now, huddled in a small consultation room at Mercy Hospital in Stonerock, Tennessee, waiting to hear the diagnosis of his five-year-old daughter while sitting next to the wife who'd left him...well, Sam's nerves were flat-out shot.

Dr. Benson displayed a glossy page with several images. "You can see on Marley's CT scan that everything appears to be in good shape."

Actually, Sam couldn't see that because he was an architect, not a doctor.

"If things are good, then why did you bring us in here?" Tara asked. "I want to be with my daughter."

His wife sat too close, smelled too good and was clutching the strap of her purse like it was the only thing keeping her grounded. If they were a normal couple, he'd reach out and take her white-knuckled hand to offer support. If they were a normal couple, they would've driven here together when the school called and said that Marley had hit her head when she fell from the playground equipment at a party on the last day of a summer school program.

If they were a normal couple, he wouldn't have divorce papers waiting for his signature just below where his wife had already signed away their marriage.

"Marley is a lively little girl. I can tell from the time I spent with her doing my assessment. This fall could have been much worse." Dr. Benson shifted his focus from Sam to Tara. "A head trauma can cause multiple issues and some aren't seen by simply looking at the outward appearance."

"Just say it," Sam demanded. "What's wrong with my daughter?"

Technically, she was his adopted daughter. When he'd met Tara, Marley had just turned two. He'd fallen in love with both raven-haired beauties and quickly made them his family. Marley was his in every single way that mattered. Even if Sam and Tara's marriage was one signature away from the end, Marley was still his.

Sam couldn't figure out what was actually wrong

with her, though. He'd seen Marley, he'd talked to her. She showed him where her head hurt and the scrapes on her legs from the fall.

She'd been talking just fine and even asked when they could go home. So why the cryptic chat in private?

"I consulted with another colleague," the doctor went on. "We both believe Marley has retrograde amnesia."

The doctor's words took a moment to sink in. Sam wasn't sure what retrograde amnesia was, but he sure as hell knew the term *amnesia*. Marley had fallen off the top of a slide and hit her head on the pole holding up the ladder. Amnesia? Wasn't that a term used in movies? This was real life—this was his *daughter's* life.

"Amnesia?" Tara's whispered question had an underlying hint of denial. "But I talked to her. She called me Mommy and talked like she always does. She didn't seem confused."

The doctor nodded. "She's not right now. Retrograde amnesia is where the patient is missing a portion of time, so unless you asked her about something specific, she wouldn't know she was missing the memory. RA patients have retained information in their minds. In Marley's case she knows her parents, where she lives, her favorite toy. Those are all things that have been a constant in her life. But she's not aware she's finished kindergarten. She remembers being in preschool, which isn't part of the camp she's in today. She remembers the two of you marrying—or, at least, the pictures from that day and memories you've discussed with her since she was little. She's chatted quite a bit with me, but from listening, she's lost the last year of her life."

An entire year? His daughter was only five years old and she'd lost twenty percent of her life? How did something as common as a fall on the playground result in his baby girl being robbed of her memories?

Sam struggled to wrap his thoughts, his emotions, around this moment. How the hell had they landed here? How had he and Tara gone from the happiest, most loving couple to being separated and now dealing with Marley having amnesia? Life could spin out of control in an instant and he was more than done with the ride.

An accident of his own had stolen the life he and Tara had created. Little by little, the addiction chipped away until he'd left Tara no choice but to leave and protect their daughter.

And now look where they were. Him clean and sober for a year, holding down a steady job he was proud of, and desperately wanting his family to be whole again. He hadn't even been sure that was possible, but now his baby girl...

"We want another opinion," Sam stated, shifting in his seat.

Damn it. He'd gotten his life together; he'd overcome addiction and was ready to fight for his family, to get them back to where they used to be before pills destroyed them. He might have lost Tara, but that didn't mean he was abandoning them. He planned on being a provider, damn it. He would make this up to them, even if he'd killed any chance of being Tara's husband again.

Panic stirred at the thought of his sweet Marley totally unaware of what she faced. His sole purpose and goal over the past year had been to repair his life, Tara and Marley's lives. How the hell did he fix this? He was her father. He was supposed to fix things when she got hurt or was sad.

"Wanting another opinion is understandable." Dr. Benson slid the images into Marley's medical folder. "As I stated before, I consulted with one of my colleagues and his prognosis was the same. I'm a parent myself, so I understand the concern and the fear."

"Does she know?" Sam asked, swallowing his own worry so he could focus on finding a quick fix. Unfortunately, he had a sinking feeling there was no quick or easy fix. This sounded like something that could only be healed by time.

Dr. Benson shook his head. "I wanted to discuss everything with the two of you and let you figure out how to tell her. The news would be best coming from the people she's closest to."

Sam glanced to Tara. Tears slid down her face as she stared at the doctor. She'd shed too many tears because of him and his selfish actions. He didn't even remember the last time he saw her smile, and every single time she hurt, it gutted him.

Unable to watch her suffer alone, Sam reached across for her hand, which she quickly pulled away. The rejection wasn't a surprise. Knowing Tara would rather face this unknown future with Marley's medical issue than accept his touch stung… but why had he expected her to let him in? He deserved nothing.

"What can we do for her?" Tara swiped at her damp cheeks before smoothing her wavy hair behind her shoulders. "How can we make her memories return?"

"You're going to want to make her life as stress-free as possible," Dr. Benson stated simply. "Right now she's floating around the time frame when she was about three or so. She's a happy girl. When I asked about her home life to see what she recalled, she mentioned her dog, Daisy, that the two of you just got married and that you guys were planning a beach vacation."

Sam's heart sank. She'd been at the altar with them when they married—that was one thing he'd insisted on. Her dog had been hit by a car when

Sam hadn't fixed the back door and she'd gotten out and darted after a stray cat. And that beach vacation was supposed to have taken place right after she turned four. Everything happy in her memory bank had been tarnished. He'd done that. He'd ruined her childhood.

When pills had overtaken Sam's life, taking priority over his family, and he'd missed her fourth birthday party, Tara had officially had enough and kicked him out. There had gone the loving beach vacation as a family.

"I'd say with a stable home life and doing what you always did as a family, Marley will have a better chance at regaining her memories. But whatever was going on when she was three will have to be going on now, I'm afraid. Slowly her memory should return, but the mind is so complex, we just don't know."

Sam's thoughts tumbled into each other as he tried to figure out exactly what all of this meant. Dr. Benson had no clue he and Tara were separated, and at the time Marley was three their family hadn't quite started falling apart yet. So as far as his daughter was concerned, her parents were still happily married and Daisy the faithful dog was alive and well.

Damn it.

Perhaps they could find a new Daisy dog for her. But the marriage? He didn't want to make things more difficult for Tara. If she was constantly questioned…it would make a bad situation even more uncomfortable. There was no way he would make her life that much more unbearable. From the moment he'd gotten clean and sober, Sam had vowed to do whatever he could to make Tara and Marley's lives better…even if that meant he wasn't living under the same roof…though that was exactly what he wanted. More than anything.

Tara might have pushed him out of their home, out of the marriage, but that act of tough love had been the exact slap in the face he'd needed to make him seek help. Losing his family, his *life*, had utterly destroyed him.

Sam had always heard the term *rock bottom*, and losing everything he held precious had no doubt been his bottom. Through counseling, he realized now that no one could heal him until he actually wanted to be healed. Damn, he'd been so selfish for so long.

Would they all be in this predicament if he hadn't turned to pills to cope with life? Would his daughter be fine?

He honestly had no reason to think this was his fault, but he needed to place the blame somewhere and his shoulders already carried the brunt of the load of his screwed-up life.

"When can I take her home?" Tara asked, cutting into his wandering thoughts.

I. Not we.

Sam wasn't about to correct her, not here. But there was no way he'd let either of the ladies he loved go through this without him. He would be the foundation in this family once again and he'd make damn sure Marley got the best care and recovered fully. Clearly, Tara didn't want him around, but that was too damn bad. Not only did Marley need taking care of, but Tara couldn't do all of this alone—and she shouldn't have to.

Above his need to prove to Tara that he was a different man, their little girl and her condition had to come first. Those initial goals after becoming sober were now completely different. Sam hated the thought of telling his innocent daughter what had happened. She was so young. How could she possibly understand what all of this meant? He was thirty-six and could barely wrap his mind around this whole amnesia thing himself.

"We will keep her here overnight," Dr. Benson told Tara. "One of you can stay with her and she will be dismissed first thing in the morning, provided there are no surprises. I scheduled a repeat CT scan for later tonight to double-check for swelling. I suspect it will be clear, but with children and head traumas, unexpected things pop up and I'm taking precautions."

"I'll stay," Tara stated.

Again, Sam wasn't going to argue. Besides, Marley would want her mother here. But that didn't mean he wouldn't make provisions for when they returned home. Already he'd started planning and plotting.

Sam would make sure Marley got her memories restored, then he'd prove to Tara that he'd changed and he was able to provide for his family. Life might have knocked him down, but he was coming back now, stronger than ever.

Chapter Two

"Can I have ice cream?"

Tara stepped inside her two-story cottage, ushering Marley ahead of her. "Let's shoot for a good breakfast first and getting you settled."

The hospital had just started coming around with breakfast trays but the second Marley had gotten her discharge papers, they'd been out of there. Tara wanted to make her daughter breakfast at home; at least that would feel like getting some normalcy in this waking nightmare.

Sam came in behind her and closed the door. He carried a bundle of balloons with a bear that Marley's camp had sent to the hospital. He also held the overnight bag he'd thoughtfully packed and brought to her since she'd been staying all night. The fact he brought her a phone charger, the paperback from her nightstand, a brush, some comfortable clothes…

Part of her warmed at the idea of his trying to care for her. But now he was in her home, what used to be their home. Sam's affection for her had never been the issue. He could care for her and still not put their lives first. She wasn't taking him back, would never take that risk again, and now sure as hell wasn't the time to even think of such things.

Tara couldn't concentrate on her estranged husband or the mixed emotions she still carried around. She didn't want to think about how attentive he'd been all evening in the hospital, then showing up early this morning because he didn't want them to be alone and he'd wanted to speak to the doctor in person.

He'd also insisted on following her and Marley home. He'd pulled her aside and told her he'd talked to his boss and was taking most of the next week off work. They still hadn't told Marley anything was wrong with her memory. They'd agreed to get her home, get her settled and play things by ear. They didn't want to worry her more than necessary.

And that's precisely what Tara needed to focus on—her daughter's recovery. Because if Tara let her fears and the unknown ending to this diagnosis consume her, she'd collapse into Sam's arms and cling to the fairy tale that she'd once believed they had.

Falling into her husband's arms was the last thing she should do. They were over. She'd made that clear when she'd kicked him out the night of Marley's fourth birthday when he'd come home after missing the party. She could tell he'd been using and that had been the proverbial straw that broke the camel's back.

She'd wanted to help him. Of course she had; she was his wife. More important, she was a counselor. She'd offered him multiple names to contact, but he hadn't wanted to help himself, so there was nothing she could've said or done. Her family, her marriage couldn't stay intact if only one person held everything together.

Over the past year since their separation, though, he'd checked himself into rehab in Knoxville, gotten clean and made no bones about the fact he wanted to make up for the man he'd been. He wanted to show her and Marley that he could take care of them. He'd even told her he didn't blame her for pushing him away, but he wasn't going to ignore his duties as their provider.

Why did he have to make things so difficult?

Case in point…the unsigned divorce papers. If he'd sign those then maybe she'd feel free, but as things stood now, she wasn't free and she didn't want him to think for even a second that she couldn't manage on her own.

"I went to the store."

Sam's words pulled her from her thoughts. He stepped around Tara and picked Marley up; her squeal echoed through the foyer.

And just like that, Tara's memories flooded through. She had no clue where Marley's mind was, but Tara couldn't ignore the rush of emotions that accompanied this entire déjà vu scene.

"Your favorite strawberry ice cream is in the freezer and I'm making tacos for dinner, Marmaid."

He always called her Marmaid for her love of the ocean and mermaids, plus her name. Only Sam called her that…the special bond between father and daughter couldn't be severed. Unlike Sam and Tara's marriage.

Tara stood in place, watching Sam's retreating form, remembering all those times he'd carried Marley around while shopping, at the annual carnival, when she'd fall asleep on the couch and he'd taken her up to bed.

Tara desperately wished she could erase her own memories of the past year. Maybe then this constant ache deep in her chest wouldn't be so all-consuming. Just because she'd pushed him away in a tough-love moment to make him focus on getting they'd married, turning one of the bedrooms into a giant adjoining bath.

But as soon as she crossed the threshold to her room, she froze. A large, black, menacing suitcase sat on her bed. She knew that suitcase; she'd *bought* that extra suitcase for their beach trip that never came to fruition.

Dread curled low in her belly.

He wouldn't.

Tara knew exactly what she'd find in the luggage he'd parked on her side of the mattress. As she crossed to her king-sized bed, she attempted to take in deep, slow breaths, but nothing calmed her nerves.

With a shaky hand she reached for the zipper. She flipped the top and stared at perfectly folded jeans, tees, underwear, running shoes…

Sam's things. They even smelled like him. That familiar woodsy scent wafted up and assaulted her senses, making her stomach clench with…what? She couldn't even label her emotions at this point—there were simply too many.

Blowing out a sigh, Tara closed her eyes and dropped her head between her shoulders. This was not happening. It couldn't be happening. No way was Sam staying here. He could come and go as often as he wanted. She'd certainly never denied him any involvement with Marley. On that they had always agreed. But he would not be staying in her home while Marley recovered.

Surely he wasn't using Marley's condition to try to come back? He hadn't signed the divorce papers, so did that mean he thought there was a chance? He hadn't made a move on her since coming out of rehab; he hadn't tried to push his way into their lives. In all honesty, he'd been the perfect gentleman. She hadn't known what to expect. They'd been so passionate early in their relationship so now things always seemed odd…strained.

Tara bounded down the stairs and headed toward the kitchen. Sam stood at the island with a bowl, eggs and bread. Marley was on her knees on a stool beside him. This had been their thing. Sam had always been a phenomenal cook—that was one of the many ways he'd captured her heart. But when he started incorporating Marley into the prep work and she eventually graduated to using the stove with assistance, Tara had utterly melted.

Even though Marley had been a toddler when she'd started helping, she'd actually mastered measuring and mixing.

"Hey," he said, smiling across the room at her. "We're making French toast. Interested?"

"He said no ice cream for breakfast." Marley pouted as she cracked an egg into the bowl.

Tara offered her daughter a smile but shook her

head. "Actually, I need to speak to your daddy for a minute."

Sam's eyes snapped to hers, but his own smile didn't diminish. How could this look so right, so painstakingly familiar, yet every bit of this morning be so devastatingly wrong? She couldn't handle him in their kitchen, like this was old times, let alone stay for...however long he'd intended. His suitcase had been crammed full. They'd bought the house together when they'd married, but he'd given it to her in the divorce. Still, this was their space and memories flooded her now that he was back.

Sam grabbed a dish towel and wiped his hands as he circled the island. "Just crack the eggs and I'll be right back so we can start dipping the bread."

Marley began humming as she cracked another egg. Tara pulled in a deep breath, telling herself not to explode because yelling or getting upset would get them nowhere. Still, she had to make Sam understand he simply couldn't stay. She had to remain firm on this for her sanity. Falling into their pattern of her enabling his actions would only lead to disaster and leave her where she'd crawled her way out of.

But she was still enabling, wasn't she? Just like she'd covered for him when he'd been using. Pretenses...they were an ugly thing to try to keep up.

Tara went up the stairs and into the bedroom, well aware he was directly behind her.

"What the hell is this?" she asked, pointing to the bed.

With a casual shrug, he crossed his arms over his massive chest. "My suitcase."

She willed herself to find patience. "Why is it on my bed?"

Casual as you please, Sam leaned against the door frame. "I'm staying."

"No, you're not."

He couldn't. She'd barely gotten used to this house without him. Having him here would be too cruel and dealing with Marley on top of that…she simply didn't think she could handle all the emotions at once.

The irony that she counseled people yet couldn't even get her own life in order was not lost on her.

Sam pushed off the frame and took one slow step at a time until he'd closed the space between them. Tara concentrated on her breathing; it was better than focusing on those gray eyes that seemed to look right into her soul.

"The doctor said Marley lost the last year of her life," he reminded her in a low tone that had Tara shivering. "He said to make her life stress-free and as normal as possible. In her mind, we're married and we all live here. Do you want to explain to her why I don't? She doesn't know about the separation."

Tara gritted her teeth as she sank onto the bed

next to the threatening suitcase. She hadn't thought of that part. She'd been too worried about how to help Marley remember to even think about the time frame her mind was trapped in. And perhaps she'd selfishly feared how she'd ever let Sam back into her home, into her bed, without losing her mind or her heart all over again.

Sam squatted in front of her, placing his hands on her knees. Tara tried to shift, but he held firm.

He hadn't touched her, not like this, in well over a year. She'd be lying if she said she hadn't missed those strong hands on her. How could she be torn in so many different directions and still keep pushing forward through life? She had no idea what she was doing and how she was holding things together.

"This isn't about us right now," he told her. "As much as I want to make everything up to you and make you see that I'm a different man, this is about Marley. She needs her mom and dad, and I will not fail her or you ever again."

Tears burned Tara's eyes. She wished like hell he meant those words, but she'd heard them before. Over and over he'd promised he wouldn't fail her… but he always did.

"You can't live here," she whispered through the emotions.

Sam rose to stand above her, forcing her to tip

her head up to meet his gaze. He propped his hands on his hips; the muscle in his jaw clenched.

"We're going to be married and living together like one big happy family for Marley's sake. So I'm not only living here," he informed her. "We're sleeping in the same bed."

Chapter Three

"Where's Daisy?"

Marley's question broke through the awkward tension filling the kitchen. Breakfast had been mostly Marley chattering and Sam and Tara dancing around each other without speaking.

Now Tara rinsed off the dishes and sat them on the counter for Sam to put into the dishwasher.

"When you had your accident, Daisy had to go to the boarder."

The lie slid out of Sam's mouth and sounded so convincing. Tara couldn't help but wonder how easily he'd lied to her in the past and if he ever truly felt guilty about deceiving. But, for now, Tara didn't want to break her daughter's heart, so she was going to go along with Sam and see how things went. Every day, every moment, would be playing things by ear.

"When can we go get her?"

"We'll see, honey," Tara chimed in. She set another glass on the counter. "Let's focus on you healing, okay?"

Still seated at the table, Marley propped her chin on her hand. "What's wrong with me? My head hurts."

The swollen red knot on her forehead near her hairline was a constant visual reminder of how quickly their lives had changed. Tara couldn't stand the thought of something happening to her daughter. Hadn't their family been through enough? There was only so long she could be strong and she truly feared she was edging closer to her breaking point.

Tara threw a glance to Sam, but his attention and concern were directed at Marley.

"We don't want you to worry, but you do deserve the truth," he said. "Let's go into the living room and talk. Okay?"

Without waiting for a response, Sam scooped Marley up and airplaned her along the narrow hallway. Tara followed them in time to see him safely land her on the oversized sofa like he had countless times before. Usually for movie or game night, but that was just another bond those two shared. Be-

his gaze over top of Marley. Sam shook his head and held her eyes until she nodded in agreement.

Perhaps they shouldn't say anything too upsetting because Marley wouldn't completely understand the ramifications of memory loss. It wasn't as if *amnesia* was an everyday term they tossed around.

Regaining the past year's memories on her own was the best way for Marley to heal, according to the professionals. Letting everything happen in a natural way would be less traumatizing…or so her doctor said.

Still, Tara had endured enough lies to last a lifetime and keeping this to herself was like a knife to her heart. She loathed lies and liars…yet here she was.

Marley's eyes darted between them. "Does that mean I can ask for something and you guys will get it for me?"

"Excuse me?" Tara asked.

"I'm supposed to be happy, right? Can I get a pet iguana? They're scaly, which kinda reminds me of a mermaid. I'll name him Ralph and he can sleep in my room."

Sam laughed and the low, familiar sound had Tara shifting in her seat. She'd missed that laugh and suddenly realized it had been too long since she'd heard it—and even longer since they'd sat like this as a family.

Pretending was most likely going to be their new norm.

"Don't press your luck," Sam told Marley as he tickled her belly. "But, seriously, if you start hurting more than usual, if you feel dizzy or nauseous or anything feels weird, you need to tell your mom or me so we can help. Got it?"

Marley nodded. "So if Ralph is a no, then maybe I could have ice cream? I ate my breakfast."

The no was on the tip of Tara's tongue, but Sam piped up. "Sure," he said. "If there was ever a time for breakfast dessert, I'd say it's today. In fact, I'll get three bowls of it. You ladies stay right here."

He was up and gone, leaving Tara speechless. This was the most interaction she'd had with him in person since she'd kicked him out. Though *kicked him out* was such a harsh term for what had actually happened. There had been tears, there had been pleading, there had been words said neither of them meant along with a broken back door. Ultimately Sam had walked out with one small bag of clothes.

He'd sent Gray to pick up the rest of his stuff while Sam had been in rehab. Seeing his side of the closet so bare had taken some getting used to—she still wasn't sure she was accustomed to the sight.

Over the past year Sam had texted her, called, left notes and flowers. He'd sent Marley flowers, as well, and she had always displayed them on the nightstand right next to her bed. She wasn't naive.

She knew he wanted their life back, but hearts weren't so easily mended. In theory, having a whole family again sounded picture perfect, but reality proved to be a different story.

Tara would never admit to anyone that she still had each and every note Sam had mailed—yes, mailed—or put under her windshield wiper over the past year. They were in a neat, orderly stack in the top drawer of her dresser.

When she'd received the first note, she'd wanted to shred it and throw it away because even seeing his handwriting had been too painful. But she couldn't bring herself to get rid of it because, as much as she wanted to hate Sam, she knew addiction wasn't a choice. He certainly hadn't chosen to get hurt and have a physician prescribe something so addictive. Yet she'd had to let him go in order to save him.

"Are you okay, Mommy?"

Tara turned her attention to Marley and smiled, though her throat burned with emotions. "Better now that you're home."

"Is Daddy okay? You guys seem kinda sad."

Why were kids so in tune with their surroundings? Tara could tell Marley eight times to get her shoes on in the morning for school and her daughter would still shuffle around in her socks until the last minute. Yet here she was, picking up on the tension between her parents without a word being spoken on the topic.

Tara would have to work harder because, as much as she hated to admit it, Sam had been right. They had to pretend to be happily married, just like they had been.

Oh, they'd been so happy. They'd been that sickening couple who held hands in public, who sent lovey-dovey texts throughout the day, who woke up holding each other after making love and falling asleep in each other's arms. They'd had their occasional disagreements, but nothing they hadn't been able to overcome.

Until addiction crept in and they couldn't overcome.

"Mommy?"

Tara smoothed Marley's hair away from her face and tapped on her daughter's nose. "What do you say we binge-watch your favorite movies all day? We'll have your favorite foods, too."

"Well, Dad is already making tacos, so that only leaves pizza for lunch."

"Pizza it is," Sam stated, coming into the room juggling three bowls of strawberry ice cream. "I'll go out and get the stuff and you can help me make it."

"Deal," Marley squealed as she took her ice cream. "Are both of you off today?"

Sam's eyes met Tara's. He offered a smile and a wink. "I took time off to be with my family."

Those last two words nearly gutted Tara. Sam seemed a little too settled into this temporary role and they'd only been faking it a few hours. How would she survive the rest of this farce?

More important, what would happen when Marley remembered that her father didn't actually live here anymore? How would she react to reliving her dog dying, her father leaving? The first time had been crushing to her sweet girl. She'd had nightmares, worried something would happen to her daddy because he wasn't home where he should be. Tara had just gotten Marley sleeping through the night again.

Tara didn't like the lies already mounting. Nothing about this was okay. Nothing.

After they finished their ice cream, Tara sent Marley to her room to get her favorite pillow, blanket and stuffed animal for movie time. Once she was out of earshot, Tara crossed to the mantel and adjusted some of the photos to give her hands something to do.

"I lived with half-truths and flat-out lies for too long," she started. "I don't like this, Sam."

His boots shuffled on the hardwood floor and she tensed as he moved closer. But he didn't reach for her.

"I don't like lying to her, either," Sam agreed.

"But we have to trust the doctors. Telling her about an entire year will only confuse her and hurt her even more. Do you want her to relive that all over again? And then again when she really remembers it?"

Tara pulled in a deep breath and turned to face him. "She'll have to relive it at some point and I think it's better coming from us than to have her smacked in the face with a blindsided thought."

"Not today." He took another step forward until he was too close. "Today, let's be the family she needs."

"And the family you want?"

The muscles in his jaw clenched. "I can't change the past, Tara. But I can sure as hell make the future better for all of us."

She'd never heard him speak with such conviction. Before he'd entered rehab, Sam had begged her to give him another chance, but she'd been all out and knew if she didn't push him away, he'd never get better. She simply couldn't risk letting him in again. Not into her heart, not into her bed.

Since he'd gotten out of rehab, he'd been the epitome of a gentleman and she wasn't sure if that pleased her and made her life easier or if it irritated the hell out of her because she couldn't figure out his angle. She thought he wanted her back, but he'd never said the words. He was just always present in one way or another.

Damn it. Her nerves were utterly shot.

"You need to sign those papers."

Sam opened his mouth, but Marley came into the room and dropped her stuff right at their feet.

"Can we watch cooking shows instead of movies?" she asked, looking between her parents, completely oblivious to the turmoil.

Well, she hadn't been oblivious. Marley knew something was up, but Tara vowed to make sure her daughter didn't suspect anything was wrong from here on out.

"Of course," Sam replied. "Then maybe you can make dinner."

"No way. You promised me tacos and I want corn cakes to go with it."

Sam ruffled Marley's hair. "You're lucky I love you."

And he did. Above all else, Sam loved Marley like she was his very own. He had from the moment he'd come into their lives. Even during his treatment, he'd made sure Marley knew he would be okay.

But he couldn't be the man she'd married. He would never be that man again and for that reason alone Tara had had to come to grips with the fact they were over.

Playing house was not helping her already battered heart and this was only the beginning.

Chapter Four

"Where's the picture when we were skiing?"

Sam stilled in the recliner across the room from Marley. Tara had gone into the other room to call Kate and Lucy since they kept texting and were worried.

"Which one?" he asked, knowing full well which photo she referred to.

There was only one that had been displayed on the mantel before. The ski trip had been one of their first getaways as a family.

Marley paused the television show as the chef set the dessert on fire. Sam watched as she slid from her makeshift bed on the sofa and crossed to the mantel. The same photos Tara had fiddled with earlier were spread across the top of it. Sam had noticed some were missing, but he hadn't said a word earlier. This was no longer his house, and as much as his obvious absence hurt him, he had no right to question Tara. She'd had to move on; she'd had to cope however was best for her.

"It always sat right here." Marley pointed to a spot where a decorative black lantern now sat. "It's my favorite family picture because we had that lady take it right after we got to the top of the mountain and you had to hold on to me so I didn't fall off the lift. Remember, Dad?"

He remembered. He recalled every single detail of their trip. His addiction hadn't swallowed his life at that point and his family had been whole and happy. They'd taken a spontaneous trip to the mountains and Tara and Marley had taken to the snow like champs. He, on the other hand, had not only hurt his backside by falling so many times, his ego had taken a hit, as well.

"Sometimes Mommy likes to rearrange things," he explained. "I'm sure it's here somewhere."

Marley crossed to him. When she climbed onto his lap, it took all of Sam's strength not to lose it. He'd seen his daughter since the separation, she'd stayed over at his apartment multiple times. But he hadn't been in this chair, in this house, cuddling with his girl.

"Can we go get Daisy now? I miss her."

Well, that was going to be a problem.

Sam smoothed her long dark hair from her face. His little girl was going to be a stunner when she grew up—just like her mother.

"Your mom and I will talk in a bit. Why don't you rest here on the sofa without the television?"

When her lip came out and she attempted those puppy-dog eyes, Sam squeezed her close to his chest. "Nice try, but you are recovering and rest is important. Your mom and I will be here, but we have things to discuss so we'll stay in the kitchen."

Marley eased back, her big blue eyes locked onto his. "Is something wrong, Dad? You and Mom seem weird."

Marley had always been smart and mature for her age, something he'd always been so proud of. "We're worried about you. We want you to feel better and make sure you don't fall off the playground equipment again."

Her brows drew in. "I don't remember falling."

Of course she didn't. While they weren't telling her the events of the past year, they had discussed how she'd gotten the knot and the headache.

"That may be best," he told her. "But why don't you rest. Okay? Maybe we can go to the park later."

"After we pick up Daisy."

Something came over her face as she glanced to the front door, then to Sam. Her brows drew in and her chin quivered.

"What is it, sweetheart?" he asked, patting her gently.

"Daisy," she murmured as tears filled her eyes.

Sam's heart clenched.

"She isn't coming back, is she?"

He wanted to lie and tell her Daisy was fine, but he couldn't bring himself to lie now that she had figured it out. "She's not. I'm sorry, baby."

Marley flung her arms around his neck, and warm tears landed on his bare skin as he comforted her with a strong hug. He held tight, letting her deal with her emotions however she needed to.

"I don't know what happened to her." Marley's tearful, muffled voice came from the crook of his neck. "I just remembered a flash of her going to the back door, but the door was stuck and I had to take her out the front, but she ran off without me."

Another layer of guilt because Sam had been supposed to fix that door. There was a spot on their rear porch where they'd hooked Daisy so she could walk into the side yard and onto the porch and to her bed near the porch swing. But the door had been stuck that day and Sam hadn't gotten it fixed... Instead, he'd gone and gotten his own fix.

Marley had let Daisy out the front door, but the gate hadn't been closed and the dog had chased a cat and been hit by a car.

Sam recalled that same back door was the one he'd nearly ripped off the hinges the day he'd left. A few days after Tara had kicked him out, he'd been sober enough to come by and fix it while he knew she'd be at work.

He'd sanded it down and repaired it, but it was still the same door. It didn't stick anymore, but he still hated that damn thing and he hated even more that his innocent daughter was sobbing in his arms yet again over the loss of her beloved pet.

"We'll get a new dog," he promised her. He probably should discuss this with Tara, but right now, Sam would promise Marley anything to get her to stop crying. "You really need to rest and we can talk about Daisy later. But you've had enough trauma for one day."

Marley eased back and sniffed as she nodded. "My next dog will have to be named Daisy."

Sam smiled as he framed her delicate face and swiped her tears away. "Name her anything you want."

He said nothing more as she slid off his lap. Marley made her way to the couch and cozied up into a ball before Sam slipped from the room. He hoped she could rest and not lie there and cry, but he would be checking in on her shortly to make sure.

Sam eased the pocket doors shut to help drown out some of the noise. They were one of the things he loved about this old cottage they'd lived in. The charm of this home they'd found together, combined with the stylish way Tara always kept each room decorated, always made Sam feel like this was a sanctuary—*their* sanctuary.

His bare apartment didn't come close to feeling like a home or looking as amazing as this house.

Sam stepped into the kitchen just as Tara sat her cell on the table. She offered him a forced smile and he hated that he'd done this to her. Hated that he'd taken the genuine smile from her lips, taken the light from her eyes.

"She's resting," he said, nodding toward the living room. "But she just remembered Daisy isn't here anymore. She doesn't know how she died, but understandably Marley is pretty upset."

"Of course she is. Damn it, I don't like this," Tara repeated. He'd lost count of how many times she'd said that since being given the doctor's advice. Tara left no room for questions on where she stood regarding their opinions.

Tara rubbed her forehead, then raked her hand over her face. Despite the fact that Sam found his wife stunningly beautiful at all times, he couldn't deny how exhausted she appeared. She had to be in a rough position, worried about Marley and having the one man she couldn't stand the sight of back in her house.

He couldn't blame her. There had been days he couldn't stand the sight of himself, either. But then he'd healed, he'd started taking a whole new outlook on life. And he was damn well going to keep moving forward until he was proud of himself again.

Without thinking, Sam took a step and started to reach for her. He hesitated, his hand in the air between them. Tara glanced from his extended arm to his eyes. Her silence was more of a green light than he'd experienced in a year.

Slowly he reached for her, feathering his fingertips across her face. Her eyes remained locked onto his and he wasn't sure if either of them had taken a breath.

"Sam."

He said nothing as he slid her hair behind her ear and left his hand right there, right at the edge of her jawline where she had a sensitive spot.

"I know you don't want me here and I promise not to make things difficult." Yet he couldn't stop himself from touching her. "Just because we're getting divorced doesn't mean I don't care. You're tired, Tara."

"I'll rest when she's better." Her bottom lip quivered a second before she glanced away. "I appreciate you being here for her, though."

Anger bubbled within him.

"Where did you think I'd be? She's my daughter."

Tara shook her head. "She is, but—"

"Are you going to go there?" he asked, crossing his arms over his chest. "Are you going to throw my past into my face? Fine, let's bring it out into the open again. I know I didn't make it to her birthday party. I'm well aware I missed bedtime stories and tucking her in more times than I can count, and I'm damn well aware of the fact that I let you down. I'll say it until you believe it, but I'm sorry. I'm sorry for the hell you had to endure."

Tara closed her eyes and pulled in a deep breath. Sam had to fist his hands at his sides to keep from reaching for her again. He was angry, but mostly at himself. No, he didn't like that she was going to bring up the wall that had divided them, but at the same time, he deserved no less.

She'd see eventually that he'd changed, that his separation from her would be his penance until the day he died. That didn't mean he'd ever give up showing her that he still cared…that he still loved her.

"I didn't mean to bring it up," she whispered, tears welling up in her eyes. "I know you worked hard to get clean, but this past year has been rough and now with Marley…"

Never in the past had he questioned when to comfort and hold Tara, and he sure as hell wasn't going to start now. They were in this together and seeing her hurt absolutely ripped his heart to shreds.

Sam closed the gap between them and wrapped his arms around her. When she stiffened, Sam gritted his teeth and cursed every blasted pill he'd ever popped, every lie he'd ever told, every tear he'd ever caused her to shed.

"You can trust me to be here for this," he murmured against her ear. "You can trust that this recovery period will be me as the foundation and the rock. I promise you."

She didn't return his hug; her arms dangled limp at her sides. But she rested her forehead on his chest. That small act proved she still cared for him. Maybe that was even worse than having her hate him. If they cared for each other, but couldn't find a way to be together, wasn't that the worst punishment of all?

"Group hug."

Sam glanced to the doorway as Marley smiled and came at them with her little arms open wide. He turned his attention back to Tara. She sniffed as she glanced up and met his eyes when Marley wrapped her arms around them…or tried to, anyway.

"I thought you were sleeping," Sam said, not taking his eyes off his wife.

When Tara remained still, Sam slid his hands down her arms and eased them onto her waist.

"Group hug," he murmured.

"I don't want to rest. I can't stop thinking about Daisy and my heart hurts." Marley eased back, then frowned. "Why is Mom crying?"

They were quite the trio of depressing emotions at the moment. Was it even possible they could all heal each other? Sam sure as hell hoped so because he didn't want to see his girls this upset over anything ever again.

"I'm so glad you're home and safe. I'm so sorry about Daisy. She loved you very much." Tara pulled away from Sam and bent to face Marley. "What do you say we paint? I bought new canvases the other day."

"Paint?" Marley seemed surprised by the request, but then her face lit up. "I love to paint."

And she was damn good at it, too, even for her age. They'd given her art lessons and she was simply a creative spirit. Sam hoped she hadn't lost the natural talent. She still had her love of cooking, so perhaps the art would be there, as well.

"Why don't you two paint? I need to step out for a bit."

Tara's eyes instantly came to his. That invisible barrier of protection immediately slid up between them. The way she looked at him, he knew exactly what she was thinking, and, damn it all, he wished she didn't immediately go to the past.

Yes, when he'd been vague about his outings in the past, he had been going to get a fix, but how long was he going to have to be reminded of that? Did her mistrust have an expiration date?

As much as he wanted to defend himself, he was tired of using words to justify his actions. From here on out, she'd have to learn to trust him or he had no hope of Tara ever moving on and fully understanding just how far he'd come. And he realized they'd never find what they once had, but he sure as hell hoped that, for the sake of Marley, they could be friends without all of the side-eye glances and questioning gazes.

"I'll paint something extra special for you, Daddy."

Sam bent and kissed the top of Marley's head. "I can't wait to see it."

Without another word, Sam turned and grabbed his keys off the counter before heading out the door. Right now he needed to concentrate on Marley, not his jumbled feelings for Tara and not the awkwardness that had settled heavy between them.

And he sure as hell couldn't focus on the fact they'd be spending countless nights together—in the same bed they'd shared as a happily married couple.

Chapter Five

The paintings were done and dried, lunch was over, Marley had napped and Sam still hadn't returned. Tara couldn't stop the thoughts swirling through her mind. How could she not revert to when he'd lived here and would disappear for hours, and sometimes days, at a time?

For all she'd seen over the past several months, he was doing his best, holding down a steady job and really putting forth an effort to be a better man. But was all of this with Marley too much for him? Did he need to find something to give him a break from reality?

Tara wanted him to remain clean, to keep rolling into another day of sobriety. She only prayed this didn't set him back. Unfortunately, when tragedy struck in an addict's life, they would occasionally slide back into using their old crutch to dull the pain. But Sam was a strong man. She truly did have faith in him and his willpower. He wanted to remain the sober man he'd worked so hard to become.

Marley sat on the sofa with her drawing pad, likely doodling another ocean or mermaid picture. Tara watched her daughter from the hallway and vowed to get her family through this without any hurt. Even though she and Sam weren't together, she would still keep her eye on him to make sure he wasn't bringing anything into the house and to make sure he stayed on the path he'd worked so hard to find.

The separation nearly a year ago had been difficult for Marley to grasp. So once that memory reappeared, Tara figured the reasoning would return. They'd been careful about how they'd explained Sam's condition, considering Marley was so young. How could anyone truly explain drug addiction to such an innocent child?

Tara and Sam had been as honest as possible, explaining that he had to go away to get better and that sometimes people could love each other but not live together or be married anymore.

Sam hadn't wanted the divorce, and obviously still didn't since the papers were lying unsigned in his apartment across town. What was the purpose of dragging this out? She'd had to muster up every ounce of her courage to go see her attorney and start the process.

Her heart had shattered that day. The last thing she wanted was to be divorced, but she hadn't seen a future for them. She worried that if she let him in he would fall down the same path and she would enable him once again. For months she'd hid his addiction, sometimes turning the other cheek because she didn't want it to be true.

Her counselor had told her that she had enabled him, but she hadn't purposely done so. There was such a fine line to walk when dealing with an addict between wanting to help them and trying to love them. Tara had to keep Sam at a distance, no matter how difficult…no matter how much her heart still ached to have him with them.

Tara crossed her arms and chewed on her bottom lip as she continued to watch her daughter. She didn't want Marley to suffer more than necessary. Growing up, Tara never knew when her parents were going to be together or living in separate places. Her father came and went so much, the revolving door became the norm.

There was no way Marley would have that lifestyle. The moment Tara discovered her pregnancy, Marley's father had vanished. When Sam came along, Tara had been so hesitant to give her heart, to share her child. But he'd been impossible not to fall for. His charm, his compassion, the way he took to Marley as if she were his own.

Tara's heart clenched at the idea that the man she'd loved was forever gone. No matter if he was clean now, he'd been changed forever. Their worlds had been changed forever.

So keeping this arrangement, with shared custody, was at least a routine they could all get used to, because if Tara opened their home and there was another setback… Tara didn't think her heart could handle another break.

The clatter of paws over the hardwood floor pulled Tara from her thoughts. That poor dog clearly couldn't get traction on—

Wait. Paws? Dog?

She spun around as a massive beast came barreling toward her, pulling Sam, who held on to the other end of the leash. Tara would have laughed at the sight if she weren't so shocked at the takeover of her home.

"What in the world?"

Tara barely got the words out before she had to plaster herself against the wall to let the animal guiding her husband by.

"Meet Daisy." Sam gave the leash a slight tug. "Daisy, sit."

Immediately the dog dropped to her butt. Tara's gaze bounced between the suddenly obedient dog and Sam. What in the world was happening here?

"Whose dog is this?" Marley asked as she moved to the new dog invading their living room. "Can I pet her?"

"Yes, you can, and this is our dog. Daisy."

Tara snorted. "This is not Daisy."

"No. Her name really is Daisy."

The monster was taller than Marley, which looked absolutely silly as she stood before the dog and patted its head.

Tara looked closer to Marley's feet and the dog's paws…and what puddled between them on the floor.

"Is that slobber?" she asked, turning her focus to Sam.

"She has a little saliva issue. You don't want to see the inside of my truck." Sam leaned over and unhooked the leash from the St. Bernard. "She's sweet and loving, and the shelter said she's great with kids, a good protector and housebroken. Her owners had to move and couldn't take her. She's four years old."

Tara shook her head and attempted to regain control of her thoughts, which was all she could control at the moment because some mammoth animal was taking up the living room.

"Why is she here?" Tara asked slowly, praying for patience.

"Daddy said we could get a dog," Marley stated,

then giggled when the new Daisy gave a big lick to the side of her face.

Sam met Tara's gaze and merely smiled. He had the audacity to smile like he was the one who should make all the decisions here. Really? Had the man not thought this moment through? Did he truly believe she'd let this fly? This was her house, not his—something he'd temporarily forgotten.

"Daddy didn't think to ask—"

"But everything is fine," Sam chimed in as he flashed a reassuring smile to Marley.

Tara narrowed her eyes and silently cursed him for lying yet again. Fine? What would happen when Marley remembered and he moved back out? Where would the dog go then?

She couldn't handle this. All the deception from the past rolling into their present situation and making her relive all those times he'd lied so easily. Granted, the doctor had told them not to reveal the memories and let them come naturally, but this was proving to be more difficult than she'd realized. Who knew how long this would last?

If there hadn't been so much dishonesty in their past, maybe Tara could have handled all of the tiny fibs a little better. But she had to deal with all of this—and likely more—for Marley's well-being.

"So we can keep the new Daisy?" Marley asked, her attention turning to Tara.

The rejection was right on the tip of her tongue.

How could she care for an animal so large? They didn't have the necessary things like bowls, food, toys, a dog bed. Getting a dog and caring for a dog were two entirely different matters.

Apparently, Sam wasn't completely reformed because he was still making rash decisions without talking to her.

"The new Daisy is staying," Sam declared with a wide smile as if he'd saved the day. "She's going to love it here."

Here. As in her house. There was the biggest, slobberiest dog standing in her living room, coating her beautiful original oak flooring with who knew what. What cleaner took care of such a mess?

Lord, give me strength.

"Where will she sleep?" Tara asked. "Because my bed is off-limits."

"*Our* bed is off-limits," Sam amended, covering her slipup. "I figured we could keep her gated in the kitchen. That way, if there's an accident, we can clean it up easy and the hardwood isn't in there to ruin."

"We have no gates, no dog bed, no dog food for this size of an animal..." Tara ticked off the list of needs, and that was all off the top of her head. What else would they need to get? Bib to catch the obvious drool issue?

"All taken care of and out in my truck." Sam bent over and tapped on the thick, purple collar with a heart tag dangling. "That's what took me so long. I found the dog, then I had to go get everything, then return to the shelter for her and do all the paperwork."

And here she'd been thinking the worst. Guilt settled heavy in her gut. Clearly, this whole playing house situation was going to be one smack in the face after another. She honestly had no clue what to do or what would be thrown her way next. One thing was certain, though—she had to be prepared for the onslaught of emotions and feelings…and needs that would come with living with Sam again.

And they hadn't even gotten to the sleeping arrangements.

Sam settled Daisy in the kitchen and left the light on over the stove. He made sure each door was locked, just like he always had when he'd lived here before. The little accent lamp they'd gotten as a wedding present sat in the corner of the living room and always remained on at night, casting a soft glow throughout.

The familiarity of the routine didn't feel wrong at all…and that was a problem. He wasn't staying; he couldn't even let his mind think that way. This was no longer his home, but while he was here, he sure as hell would make sure his family was safe.

With a final glance around the first floor, Sam mounted the steps to his room.

No, not his room anymore. His pretend room where he would pretend to be happily married to Tara and pretend that none of this was awkward and one of the most difficult things he'd ever done in his life.

Faking a loving, committed marriage to Tara was a hell of a lot more difficult than rehab had been. Because at least in rehab he'd known he was getting better and working toward becoming whole again.

At the end of this farce, he seriously worried he'd not come out unscathed.

Sam paused in front of Marley's room and peeked in. She lay peacefully on her side, hugging her favorite stuffed mermaid…the one he'd gotten her for her fourth birthday. The party he'd missed. The gift had come late, unwrapped, but she'd carried it around since that day and loved it anyway… she loved him anyway, despite his multiple stumblings.

The heart of a child was so humbling and precious. He deserved nothing, yet his daughter saw beyond everything and kept her heart open.

An entire storm of emotions rolled through him. He'd purchased that damn mermaid thinking it would make up for missing her party. Seeing it now, he wanted to rip it to shreds and forget that time of his life.

But it was remembering all those dark times, all

the valleys he'd been temporarily rooted in, that kept him pushing forward each day to be a better man, a better father.

Sam eased her door closed and turned to the room at the end of the hall. He hadn't slept here in a year. Despite being gone for so long, he could still recall the creak in the floor at the foot of the bed, the way the sunlight spilled in the window if the curtains weren't closed just right, the way he'd always thought the room smelled feminine and he wondered if his clothes would forever be embedded with Tara's floral scent.

Now he'd give anything to have that scent on his clothes, but that chapter was over in his life. Now he was lucky to have found work, considering his past. He often smelled like a sweaty guy, but he was proud of where he'd landed and he only hoped one day Marley would be proud to have him as her dad.

Tara stepped from the master bath as Sam entered the room. The bed sat between them and he simply stayed in the doorway, staring across the room at his gorgeous wife—because, damn it, they were still married. Maybe not emotionally, but legally.

"So, what do we do here?" she asked, blurting out exactly what he'd been thinking all evening. "I'm not having sex with you."

Sam stepped farther into the room. "I never expected you to, but for the sake of Marley, we will both be sleeping in this bed."

Tara quirked a brow. “For her sake?”

“She still has nightmares,” he told her. “Well, she did before all of this. If she crawls into bed and I’m sleeping on the floor or downstairs on the sofa, do you want to answer all of those questions?”

“Maybe we could lie to her. We’ve been doing it all day anyway.”

The hurt lacing Tara’s tone irritated him. Not because she was in pain, but because he hated that she was in this predicament once again. No doubt when he’d been MIA during his addiction, she’d had to lie to Marley to cover for him.

“This will get better,” he assured her as he pulled his shirt over his head. He was dead tired and wanted nothing more than to crawl into this bed and pass out. “I’m confident her memories will…”

Sam lost all train of thought at the sight of Tara staring at his exposed chest. He knew she’d spotted the new tattoo, but she didn’t say anything. Instead, her eyes held on the ink for a few moments before traveling over his exposed skin. He couldn’t deny that his ego swelled, but again, lust and physical intimacy had never been their issue.

He was just thankful she hadn’t asked about the tattoo. He wasn’t quite ready to explain its meaning to her quite yet…if ever.

“This won’t work,” she muttered. “I mean, I’m still attracted to you, but I don’t want to be.”

Sam laughed and tossed his shirt onto his suitcase in the corner. "Don't hold back. Be honest with your feelings."

Her eyes darted up to his. "You don't want me to go there."

No, he probably didn't. "This bed is big enough," he reminded her. "You won't know I'm there."

Her eyes widened as she shook her head. "Not likely, but it sounds good in theory."

She grabbed a nightgown from the dresser and went into the bathroom. Sam blew out a sigh of frustration and stripped to his boxer briefs. He could be a gentleman and put on a pair of shorts, but this was his old bed, this was his wife and, damn it, he wasn't going to be uncomfortable just because Tara was still attracted to him. Her attraction sure as hell wasn't one-sided.

Sam slid between the crisp, cool sheets and pulled the comforter up to his chest. Lacing his fingers behind his head, he stared up at the ceiling and wondered how long this night would be. Each minute would no doubt drag by at an excruciating pace.

The bathroom door opened once again and Tara didn't move farther into the room and she didn't climb into bed. Sam shifted to see what she was doing, but she merely stared at him.

"What now?" he asked.

"I've been sleeping on that side."

His side? The side he'd slept on the entire time

they were married? Interesting…and rather telling of her feelings. He really shouldn't read too much into this nugget of knowledge, but he was human and his ego had taken a beating. He was most definitely grabbing on to this and tucking it away for future use.

Tara raised a brow and continued to stare. Fine. He was flexible, so long as she didn't think he'd be on the floor or the sofa.

Sam tossed back the sheet and came to his feet. He circled the bed and Tara still hadn't moved. She wore one of those tank-style cotton gowns that hit above her knees. The outline of her body drew his eyes. He fisted his hands at his sides and forced himself to reach for the corner of the blanket. In doing so, his arm brushed hers and he couldn't ignore the tremble…from her? From him? Maybe both.

Slowly he straightened, keeping his eyes on hers. All day he'd only seen worry, a touch of fear and exhaustion. Now, staring at her, all he saw was… damn it. All he saw was desire.

"You can't look at me like that," he warned. Though he ignored the blaring horns inside his head and stepped into her, settling one hand on the dip in her waist. "That's the look that I never could turn down. That silent invitation."

"Having you here is more difficult than I thought," she admitted on a whisper.

And as much as he wanted to follow her onto that bed and forget everything that stood between them—namely a piece of paper ready to end everything—he had to respect her initial wishes. If he ever got her back, it wouldn't be because he'd used Marley's situation to do so.

Sam settled his other hand on her waist and blew out a breath. "I'm struggling, too," he confessed. "It's been too long since I touched you, Tara. But this isn't the right time."

He might not be giving in to his every desire, but he was still a man, damn it. Sam dropped his forehead to hers just as her hands came to her sides and squeezed his wrists.

"Sam, I need—"

He had no idea what she was going to say. His mouth settled over hers, cutting off her words because he needed it, too. Just a taste. Just. One. Taste.

So much need and ache consumed him. Tara's clutch on his wrists tightened as she opened her mouth, giving him greater access.

But before he could get too swept away with the memories—the good ones—and the sweet taste of his wife, Sam pulled away.

Tara stared up at him and he had to force himself to step back. Her fingertips went to her damp lips and she closed her eyes.

"I won't apologize," he told her. "We both wanted that kiss, but that's where it ends."

Brief as it had been, he had a feeling he'd still be tasting her on his lips come tomorrow.

When Tara said nothing, Sam reached for the pillow and pulled it off the bed. He turned to the end of the bed, grabbing the perfectly folded throw from the bottom. "I'll go sleep on Marley's floor."

"Sam, don't."

He stilled in the doorway, throwing a glance over his shoulder to the temptress staring at him. "If we crawl into that bed together, we'll both wake with regrets."

He'd waited so long, had prayed and pleaded to get here, but there was no way he would take advantage of the moment. Tara deserved better. Hell, he deserved better.

Sam crossed the hall and made a bed on his daughter's floor. And he didn't sleep one bit.

Chapter Six

"I kissed him."

Silence surrounded her and Tara glanced up from the table of brochures to see her very best friends, Lucy and Kate, staring at her, mouths open and eyes wide.

Yeah, maybe she should've led in with a softer opening. She was still processing everything herself, so she hadn't had time to construct an eloquent sentence.

"He's only been in your home one day," Kate stated, as if Tara needed the reminder.

They were setting up for their monthly grief meeting at the community center. The three had come together through their own hardships and discovered there was a need in this small community of Stonerock for those who had lost loved ones. They didn't focus on the loss, but rather met once a month to form an upbeat, positive atmosphere for those who were hurting.

At least this way, people could bond with others and form deeper friendships over similar hurts. The meetings over the past years had been successful and really opened an avenue of friendships for people who otherwise wouldn't have opened up and let new relationships form.

Like Lucy and Noah. They'd both lost a spouse in tragic circumstances but had come together and now had a beautiful family.

"Did you sleep with him?" Lucy asked, abruptly jerking Tara from her thoughts.

Tara shook her head and flattened her palms on the table. "No. But how on earth are we going to keep up this charade in front of Marley? He ended up sleeping in her room last night. He couldn't get out of our bedroom fast enough after we kissed."

"Why are you upset?" Kate dropped into a metal chair at the end of the table. "You wanted this divorce and now you kiss him? You're sending mixed signals. He probably hightailed it out of there before he did something you both regret."

He'd said as much on his way out the door. Still, part of her wished he'd stayed so they could've talked. The other part of her, the part that was filled with fear and worry, knew he'd made the right decision.

"The kiss wasn't supposed to happen," she defended herself. "But he didn't have a shirt on and there was a new tattoo I couldn't stop staring at. I had on my nightgown, and he stepped close, smelling so, so..."

She had no valid reason to want his mouth on hers, to dive back into that emotional pull, other than the fact she'd wanted him to kiss her and she hadn't pushed him away. It was simple, yet complicated, but she was human with emotions all over the place.

"It's okay to want to get back together," Kate said, softly. "You are human and it's not like you can just shut off your feelings."

Tara focused her attention on her friends. "I never said that. Getting back together with Sam would be a mistake."

"Playing house and not falling in love with him will be difficult," Lucy pointed out, as if falling in love with Sam was the next logical step. They couldn't even be alone in the same room at this point. So love sure as hell wasn't an option.

Tara glanced at the clock on the wall. The group would start arriving and she certainly didn't want to get into this here and now. She should've never brought up the kiss, but she'd needed to talk and

Lucy and Kate were her very best friends. She trusted them with everything.

Well, except to tell them her divorce wasn't final. She didn't want anyone to know Sam hadn't signed the papers yet. She'd wanted to be a strong woman, wanted to move on with the next chapter in her life. It had been an entire year and she still had an anchor on her, weighing her down. She had to somehow set herself free before she found herself drowning in a situation she couldn't get out of.

Not only had Sam not signed the papers, he was also living with her again and playing the doting husband and father. He made memories rush back nearly every moment. She'd barely exorcized him from each room over the past year. She'd removed pictures that hurt to look at, she'd left his side of the closet bare and the door closed. But now he flooded every part of her life again. She had her reasons for being so harsh, for being, some would say, cold.

She was saving her daughter's future. If she let him in, if he went down that path of addiction again, she didn't know if she'd have the strength to make him leave again. Because, in all honesty, she just wanted to hold him, to make his life perfect, to heal him. Isn't that what she did? She healed people who were broken…or, at least, that's what she'd devoted her career to.

One day, she hoped to have her own office and run a counseling center instead of working for someone else. She loved her job, but she wanted more control and a softer atmosphere than the sterile building where she currently worked.

"I think we need to go to Gallagher's after the meeting," Kate stated, patting her protruding belly. "Gray will hook us up. I mean, he'll hook you up with a margarita. I'll stick with lemonade."

Kate's husband, Gray Gallagher, owned the only bar in town and they often went for ladies' night or to enjoy a drink and some pub fries, sometimes a little dancing, too. Not only had Kate married her best friend, she was also expecting his child.

Tara shook her head. "I'm not really in the mood. Besides, I need to get home to Marley."

"I'm surprised you came at all tonight," Lucy responded. "Is she feeling okay?"

"She is," Tara confirmed. "The doctor stressed that we need to keep things as normal as they were when Marley believed we were all living together like one happy family. I wanted to cancel, but Sam assured me they would be fine and we had to listen to the doctor."

Kate reached over and squeezed Tara's hand, offering a soft smile. "Nobody would say a word if you wanted to slip out early and head home."

Tara wanted nothing more than to be home watching over Marley, but at the same time, she did need to do what the doctor said and she wasn't so sure being in that house, trapped with all those memories and Sam, was the best thing for her sanity right now.

"I'll stay," she stated. "We'd better get the refreshments out before everyone gets here."

Kate nodded, smoothed her shirt over her rounded belly and headed to the rear of the community center where they'd stored their goodies in a small kitchen. Lucy circled the table and propped her hip on the edge. "Why don't I bring Emma over to play?"

Tara's first response was to say yes, but then she thought of the timeline. "Marley didn't know Emma when she was three."

Kate shrugged. "Then I'll bring her over and we'll introduce them again. I can explain to Emma that Marley is having a tough time remembering so she needs to pretend they've never met. Believe me, Emma is all about acting now. She wants to try out for the local plays at the theater in town."

Tara laughed, immediately picturing sweet Emma with her wildly curly blond hair stealing the show. "I think that's a wonderful idea. Bring her over tomorrow for lunch. Who knows? Maybe seeing her will help trigger something."

Thankfully it was summer break and Tara didn't have to worry about school, teachers and other kids confusing Marley. Her accident had taken place on the last day of a summer program Tara had signed Marley up for.

When people started to wander in, Tara immediately greeted them, trying her best to get back to her normal life. She had to keep telling herself she could and would get through this difficult time. This was a grief share group, after all, so what better place for her to be? She had no clue how to deal with all of the juxtaposition of emotions. Honestly, she couldn't even name all of them at this early stage in the game.

No. None of this was a game. Having the past year wiped from her daughter's memory and having her soon-to-be-ex living with her again was very much real.

Maybe she did need a girls' night out. Perhaps purging all of her thoughts would be the therapeutic balm she needed right now. Being with her two very best friends would definitely be the comfort she needed.

There was no way she could express her fears and her concerns to Sam. He'd always been the one she'd turned to, but not since he'd shattered the trust between them.

Tara vowed after the meeting to talk with Kate and Lucy about getting together for some adult time. Even if it was thirty minutes over a quick lunch, Tara had to talk to someone about the crippling fear of the unknown where Marley was concerned…and the man who was posing as her loving husband.

* * *

"I don't like you living there again, Sam."

Sam rubbed his forehead and sank onto the bench he'd built into the deck off the back porch. Marley rode her bike on the driveway and along the sidewalk around the garage. His mother had called to check on her granddaughter and wasted no time in expressing her opinion on the situation.

"This is my family, Mom. I shouldn't be anywhere else."

"That woman didn't stand by you when you needed her and now you're back in her house."

"It's still our first house and she pushed me away for good reasons." He defended Tara. "She had to look out for herself and our daughter. If she hadn't, I don't know that I would've sought the help I needed."

His mom merely grunted before diving in for more. "You can stay in your apartment and still care for your daughter. She knows you love her."

"We're going on the doctor's orders." How many times had he already said that to her via texts and calls? "If you'd like to visit, you're more than welcome. Marley would love to see you."

"I plan on coming this weekend," his mom stated. "I didn't want to overwhelm her."

"You won't overwhelm her. She's acting like Marley." He watched as she wobbled around the garage once again with the purple bike that she'd gotten for Christmas last year. Apparently her memory had stolen the fact she had become an excellent rider. "She's had some headaches off and on, but that's to be expected. She has no idea she's missing such a large portion of her life."

He hoped the memories would return slowly and not overwhelm her all at once. When she'd woken this morning and seen him on her floor for the second night in a row, he simply explained that he'd slept in her room to keep an eye on her since her fall. The statement wasn't a complete lie. He did want to constantly watch over his little girl, but he also wanted to sleep in bed with his wife. At some point, he'd have to go into the master suite to keep up the pretense.

He wasn't going to dodge his feelings for Tara and he wasn't going to let her avoid hers, either. They were going to have to be honest and lay everything out in an attempt to move forward. Even though they weren't together, and wouldn't be when this was over, Sam still had to be completely open. Just another hard life lesson he'd learned.

Tara stepped out the back door and a big bundle of fur flew by Sam. Daisy loved the big, fenced-in yard. She ran around in circles, fur flying, tongue flapping. Sam knew Tara wasn't too pleased with him over the massive dog, but damn it, his heart had been in the right place. Didn't that count for something? Maybe he hadn't made the smartest decisions in his life, but he didn't regret putting a smile on his daughter's face.

"I'll talk to you later, Mom."

He disconnected the call and came to his feet, shoving his cell into his pocket. Tara stood at the edge of the deck and stared out across the yard toward the garage where Marley continued to make circles. She giggled when Daisy ran along beside her.

Sam crossed the yard and stepped up onto the deck he'd built only two years ago. "I'm sleeping in our room tonight."

The words were out of his mouth before he could think them through, but he was done pretending. He had to pretend with his daughter; he at least wanted to be real with his wife.

Tara continued to stare out into the yard, keeping her profile to him. "Lucy and Emma are on their way over for a visit."

Sam raked a hand along his stubbled jawline. "Did you hear me?"

Glancing over her shoulder, she merely raised a brow. "I heard you, Sam. What do you want me to say?"

He had no clue what he wanted her to say because he was in a whole new element here. But damn it, couldn't she acknowledge the issue between them? Of all people, he didn't expect her to dodge the topic. Didn't therapists make people face their fears and talk?

"I don't want this to be difficult," he told her.

She returned her attention to the yard. "It's going to be difficult no matter what we do."

"I want you to talk to me," he demanded, stepping closer to her. "You need to let me in, no matter how much you want to keep me at a distance. She's my daughter, too."

Tara turned fully to face him. "I can't let you in, Sam. No matter what else is going on, I still have to guard my heart."

Those wide eyes stared at him and the guilt consumed him once again. His penance would forever be looking at her and knowing he'd destroyed something so precious and perfect because of his selfish actions.

"I'm not going anywhere," he told her. "Even when Marley remembers, I'm going to be here for you guys. My job is secure and I'm doing better than ever. I will be your provider, and at some point, I hope a friend. Maybe you can learn to trust me again."

He turned and headed into the house before he broke down. He'd discovered in therapy that showing emotions wasn't necessarily a bad thing, but he still had some pride left. He wanted to prove to her he was a stronger man so that meant he had to hold it together whenever possible.

With Lucy and Emma coming over, he knew Tara and Marley would be fine. He needed to get out of the house for a bit and loosen this tension. It had been a hell of a week and he had a feeling things were going to get worse before they got better.

Sam grabbed his keys and decided the only place he should be was where he felt comfortable and somewhat back to normal. He headed toward the edge of town to Gallagher's. Granted, it was closing in on lunchtime and the pub didn't open until four, but Gray always kept the door unlocked for Sam.

Some people would judge Sam for hanging at a bar while recovering from his addiction, but liquor had never been a problem. He could have one beer and be done for the night.

It had been the damn pills that had ruined everything. One slip off the ladder on a construction site had resulted in an emergency room visit, followed by tests and meds and ultimately a downward spiral he'd had no control over all because he'd trusted his doctor. Who knew the doctor would become his drug dealer?

And the loss of control was the entire crux of the nightmare that had consumed him and ultimately destroyed his marriage. He'd had no control. He was a man. Men were strong, they were powerful, they fixed things in an instant and made the lives of their loved ones easier at all costs. Yet he'd been unable to deliver on any of that and he had to see that pain, that disappointment, each time he looked into Tara's eyes.

Still, he had days where he wished he could push all the pain aside and find an escape, but that was the easy way out. Sam was done doing things the easy way. He was going to work his ass off and make a better life for his family. He might have had to close his one-man architectural firm, but he'd landed a job doing what he loved and he was making great money once again.

Sam pulled into the side lot at Gallagher's and killed the engine of his truck. Having Gray in his life was priceless. No matter what had gone down, Gray had been there for him. That was the beauty of living in a small town. Yes, everyone knew your business, but for the most part, people banded together to offer their concern, and while he was healing, Tara and Marley had been looked after and loved.

Sam had gotten to know Noah quite well, too, since the man had moved to town. He was a good guy who'd come from tragedy to repair and rebuild his own life. Sam could learn a thing or two from Lucy's husband.

After locking his truck, Sam headed for the bar and stopped inside the door to adjust to the darker space. Only the lights behind the bar were on and a little peek of sunlight came in the high windows on either side of the door. Sam didn't see Gray anywhere, but he walked across the scarred wood floor and headed toward a stool. This place looked entirely different when it wasn't packed with dancing patrons and waitresses carrying trays of beers and wings.

"Hey, Sam." Kate stepped from the hallway where the offices were located. She offered a smile and rested her hands on her swollen belly. "Everything okay?"

Sam nodded. "Just needed to get out of the house for a bit. I thought you were heading over?"

"I'm going in just a bit," she explained. "Gray ran over to the next county to pick up new sound equipment. Ours is nearly shot and he found a good deal from another bar owner who is closing his business."

Kate rested her forearms on the bar. "I know I'm a hormonal pregnant woman, but I'm a pretty good listener. You caught me on a good day. I haven't cried once."

Sam laughed. "That's great to hear."

She tipped her head to the side. "Seriously. I can listen if you need."

Maybe she could, but she was also one of Tara's best friends and the conflict of interest meant it probably wouldn't be too smart for him to just open up.

"I actually didn't come here for a therapy session." Sam took a seat on a high stool. "I just wanted to give Tara some space with her friends. Things are pretty intense between us."

Kate nodded. "I can imagine. Well, actually, I can't, but I know this is difficult for all of you. It's obvious you guys still care for each other or you wouldn't be going through all of this."

Sam swallowed the first words he wanted to say. Tara didn't care for him, not like she once had. He couldn't fault her, considering he'd started them on the spiral into the depths of hell, but that didn't make the pain of rejection any less. The ache he'd found to be his new normal was always present, even more so now that he was living in his old house.

Memories threatened to take over. No matter which room he was in, Sam saw their past. The fact Tara had removed so many portraits proved how much she needed him out of her life. The visual smack to the face had been difficult to process, but he should've been prepared.

"We're living together for Marley," he stated, as if things were truly that simple. "Nothing more."

Kate pursed her lips, then blew out a sigh. She kept her gaze on his but didn't say anything as she tipped her head.

"Just say what's on your mind." Sam had known Kate long enough to know she had something to say. "I can handle it."

She turned and reached for two glasses. She filled one with water and the other with root beer. When she passed him the frothy mug of soda, he smiled.

"Thanks. Now tell me what you're dying to say."

Kate's fingers curled around her glass. "I always think events in life happen for a reason. I believe something good can come out of something tragic. And I believe that you and Tara are being given a second chance."

A second chance. Wouldn't that be nice? But he wasn't naive enough to think playing house would transform into a fresh start. He was still healing himself and regaining his ground, focusing on one day at a time.

Tara was smart not to want to take another chance with him, though he still loved her, probably more than he'd ever love anyone ever again. There would be no one else for him. Tara owned his entire heart—there was nothing else to give.

"You're a romantic now that you and Gray are engaged and expecting a baby."

Kate's smile widened. "I just want everyone to be happy."

He'd been happy once and he planned on getting there again, but the journey would be long.

Sam took a hearty drink of his root beer and sat his glass on the bar. "I don't want to keep you."

"You're not keeping me," she replied. "I was

working on invoices and payroll until he got back and I could leave. Quite the glamorous life."

The words may have been sarcastic, yet there was nothing but love. Kate had dropped everything for Gray. He hadn't asked her to, but they'd fallen in love, and from what Sam had seen, each of them would've happily tossed their old life aside for the other. But Gray's business was in the third generation and Kate didn't want him to sell. They'd been there for each other, overcoming obstacles and finding everything they never knew they wanted.

Sam couldn't help but feel a tug of jealousy. He'd had everything not that long ago. Absolutely everything he'd ever wanted…and now he was starting over.

He wasn't into mythology, but the phoenix had nothing on him. Sam had vowed a year ago to rise up from the hell he'd put himself in and nothing was stopping him. Not his broken heart, not his yearning to have his family back, nothing. He had to live for himself before he could fully live for anyone else.

Chapter Seven

"When should I start packing for the beach?"

Tara stilled, clutching her daughter's comforter as she tucked her in for the night. "The beach?"

Marley nodded, clutching her stuffed toy mermaid. "You and Daddy said we were going and I wanted to know when."

The beach trip had been canceled due to…well, her marriage and life falling apart a year ago. But, Sam had been back in the house a week and they were all going a bit stir-crazy. They needed this break.

"I can't wait to build a giant sandcastle," Marley went on as she stretched her arms vertically to show how large her castle would be. "Daddy said he'd get me new sand toys and he'd help me build it. He even said I could bury him in the sand."

Tara swallowed and attempted a smile. "Don't pack just yet."

Marley's smile instantly vanished. "We're not going?"

"Oh, of course we are."

Well, damn it. Now she had to follow through. The words slipped out before she could stop herself, but the look on Marley's face left her no choice. Was this how Sam had been sucked into the new dog?

"I need to talk to Daddy, though. Okay?"

The sweet, innocent smile returned. "Ask him if I can get a new purple suit for the trip. If not, that's okay, but I really want one."

Tara leaned over and kissed Marley's forehead before adjusting the covers. "When we go to the beach, I promise you can get a new bathing suit."

"I love you, Mommy."

No matter how old her daughter got, Tara never tired of hearing those precious words. They'd seen her through some of the toughest moments of her life.

"I love you, baby."

"Did you get your hair cut?"

Instinctively, Tara reached up and felt the ends of her hair, which was just past her shoulders now.

A little over a year ago it had been longer, but she had gotten it cut recently.

"I did," Tara stated, going along with whatever was in Marley's mind. "Do you like it?"

"I noticed it yesterday, but I forgot to tell you. I think you look pretty."

"Thank you, sweetheart." Tara came to her feet and reached over to turn off the bedside lamp. "Good night."

"Is Daddy sleeping in here again tonight?"

The words filled the darkness and Tara was glad only a sliver of light from the hall crept through the crack in the door. No way would she want her daughter to see the look in her eyes. Tara had no idea what truth her face revealed these days. She could attempt to lie, and likely convince her daughter, but her expressions always gave her away.

"We're going to be in…um, in our room tonight." Tara pulled in a deep breath. "If you need anything, come get us."

Tara slipped from Marley's room and closed the door. When she turned, she found Sam standing in the doorway to their room.

No, not their room. *Her* room. That master suite hadn't been theirs since she asked him to leave. Clearly having him back had clouded her mind, or perhaps the fact that he had been in her home for two nights had taken her to a time when everything was perfect.

He said nothing as he stared across the hallway, almost as if he were throwing down a silent challenge for her to cross to him.

Nerves swirled in Tara's belly. What could she say that hadn't already been said? He had told her earlier he would be in her bed tonight. At some point she was going to have to give in, despite what her heart told her to do.

Without a word, Sam stepped aside, allowing her the opening to pass through. Tara smoothed her hands over her simple cotton nightgown and crossed the hall. She was careful not to brush against him as she entered their bedroom.

There she went again, thinking of this as their bedroom. This could not be the new norm for them. Nothing about this was normal, and nothing about this was comfortable. She couldn't let it be because they'd all be hurt in the end.

Yet every part of her wanted to lie next to him once again and maybe just forget everything that was wrong and pretend, even if only for a moment, that everything would be okay. If she did that, there would be that fine line that could be too easily crossed. The line she had to keep firmly in place, in black and bold, because letting him in, even a little, could put them back to where they were when everything started falling apart.

Tara went to her side of the bed and folded down the blanket. The soft snick of the door behind her had her heart racing. She wished he would say something, but, at the same time, maybe silence was best.

Tara slid between the sheets and adjusted her pillows. After grabbing the book from her nightstand, she figured she could read and maybe Sam would just go to sleep.

"You always did read before bed," Sam stated as he climbed in on the other side. "What are you reading now?"

This she could do. Simple conversation, no touching or pretending they weren't both feeling torn. Books—she could talk books all day long.

"I am reading a biography about a war nurse from the late 1800s."

Sam laughed as he adjusted his covers. She tried her hardest to focus on the words and not his bare chest mere inches away—and that mysterious tattoo. But at the same time, she had to be honest, Sam's chest was far more interesting than any book she could read.

And there she was, teetering on the brink of that fine line that would plunge her into the past. She was so, so close, her toes were flirting with the edge.

"History was always your thing," Sam replied. "Do you remember when we went to Virginia and spent a whole week taking tours and seeing all the historical sites from the Civil War?"

Tara remembered. Wasn't that the whole problem with having Sam here? She remembered everything. Every single detail, every moment. Every single touch and glance. Sam was, and always had been, powerful and potent to her senses—and her heart.

"You should get some sleep." Tara gripped the edge of her book and wished he would turn off his light or put on a damn T-shirt. "You've been doing a lot and seem tired."

Sam shifted closer to her and leaned on his elbow. "Are you honestly going to act like this does not affect you?"

Tara dropped her book to her lap and turned her attention to her husband. "I have to act like this doesn't affect me. I have to keep my heart whole. It's difficult enough having you in my house, let alone in my bed. I don't want to keep rehashing the past."

"Maybe I don't want to discuss the past." Sam's dark eyes held much emotion, more than she had seen in their previous years of marriage. "Maybe I want to discuss now. Or maybe I don't want to talk at all."

Tara's heart stomped so hard in her chest, her hands grew damp. "Sam, this is not a good idea."

He continued to stare. What did he want from her? Well, she knew what he wanted, but beyond that what did he want? She had nothing left to give him. She had already given him her heart and that hadn't ended well for either of them.

"I know you're hurting," Sam said as he carefully laid his hand over hers. "I'm not trying to make this more difficult. I'm not saying I want sex—though I do want you. But I need you to know I am here, and I won't let you feel alone."

"I don't mean to be selfish with my own concerns," she amended. "I know this is hard on you, too. I can't imagine how you're coping with being here, knowing it is only temporary."

Sam nodded and released her hand as he settled against his own pillows. He blew out a sigh and placed his fingers behind his head and stared up at the ceiling. How could she not focus on this magnificent man right where he always used to be, right where she wanted him, if she were honest with herself?

He lay on his old side of the bed, the one she'd taken once he'd gone. That had been the only connection she'd had when he went away to rehab. She'd lain in that very spot and cried herself to sleep countless times and wondered if she'd made a mistake in pushing him away.

But the mistake would be letting him in, because if he faltered, she didn't know if she'd be strong enough to push him away again. Marley needed stability and Tara couldn't take the heartache again.

"I'm not worried about me," he finally said. "You

and Marley are my top priority right now. I'm on a reduced schedule for the next few weeks, and I plan on being right here through everything."

The guilt and fear inside of Tara swirled together, giving her a whole new level of anxiety. She wanted him here, yet she didn't. The internal battle she waged with herself was driving her out of her mind.

"Marley asked about the beach vacation," Tara stated, pushing her other fears aside and focusing on another. "I had forgotten we were planning the beach vacation and that would be right about the time her memories vanished."

"Then we will take her on a beach vacation."

Tara jerked her attention toward Sam; her book slid off her lap and onto the floor. "We can't just go on a beach vacation on a whim. I have obligations and clients who need me. There's only so far I can take pretending to be a happy family again."

Sam glanced at her, the slight shift only accentuating his muscular arms that stemmed from years of construction work.

"If our daughter wants to go to the beach because she remembers that we promised her, then I sure as hell am going to get her there."

Tara closed her eyes and tried to think realistically about this situation. Sam had a point, but at the same time, how far were they going to take this? How long were they going to continue this lie? Maybe if she hadn't lived through so many lies already this would be easier to deal with. And she couldn't put this all on Sam and his addiction, because she had also chosen to ignore the signs and pretend that everything was okay…pretend that with her experience and expertise she could heal him.

Perhaps if she had gotten him help earlier things would've been different. Unfortunately pride and denial had only prolonged the inevitable.

"Then let's start planning," she conceded. "Can we make it a long weekend? I really shouldn't take too much time off work since we're short-staffed as it is."

Tara honestly worried that if they spent too much time in vacation mode she would once more become the woman she was when she had fallen in love with Sam. She had to help Marley regain her memory, but Tara was quickly discovering how fragile her own heart still was.

"What are you afraid of?" Sam asked. He sat up on his elbow and faced her. "I destroyed our marriage. I broke your heart. I left Marley confused, but she can't remember. What else are you afraid of? Maybe this vacation is what we all need to start fresh."

Tara opened her mouth to correct him because there was no fresh start, but he cut her off.

"I don't mean start over with a relationship. I

know what we had is over." He paused and Tara wondered if he was struggling just as much as she was. "But we do need to start over as friends for Marley's sake and try to put the past behind us. I know those words are easy to say, but I am a different man now and I am determined to prove to you and our daughter exactly how much I care for you both. Because I do love you, no matter what happens."

Tara did not want to hear his feelings. Maybe that was harsh, but she could not listen to him say that he still loved her, no matter what level his love was. Especially considering they were in bed, half-dressed, with an attraction that hadn't faded.

"You can't say things like that to me," she whispered. "I need to get through each day, focus on Marley, focus on work and come out on the other side unscathed."

Sam stared at her for a moment, his eyes darting to her lips, then up to her eyes. "You may not want to hear what I'm feeling, but I vow to be honest with you from now on, no matter what. Sometimes the truth will be difficult, but that is something we'll both have to deal with. I'll never lie to you again."

She had heard that before. Each and every time he'd promised she'd wanted to believe him, and she'd found out it wasn't the truth.

"I will start researching for the trip tomorrow."

Tara reached over and turned off her bedside lamp. "We need to get some sleep."

As if she could sleep with him so close. Even though she had kicked him out of her house, she had felt the void in her heart just as much as the void in her bed. Having him around brought up too many memories, both good and bad.

She adjusted her covers and slid beneath them. Her foot brushed against the coarse hair on his leg. She stilled; her breath caught. Once upon a time such a simple gesture would lead to more touching. Now she didn't know what to think or even how to react.

"I'm sorry you cringe when you touch me."

Tara's heart sank. "I never want you to think that touching you bothers me. But I haven't had a man's touch in a year and you're so familiar, but..."

She hadn't meant to let that revelation out. Not that she had been looking and not that she was interested in any other man. Sam had been it for her and she wasn't sure she wanted to do love again. Besides, they were still married and she would never go against her vows.

"I've missed your touch, too," Sam whispered in the dark.

Silence settled between them. Beneath the covers his hand found hers and he slowly laced their fingers together. She closed her eyes and bit her lips, trying not to cry or tell him she'd ached for him.

"Good night, Tara."

Tears pricked her eyes at the simple gesture of his hand in hers. She had seen the hunger in his eyes earlier, she knew that he still wanted her, but he was using restraint and putting her needs first.

The problem was she had no clue what her own needs actually were. Because the female side of her wanted to forget everything and let him do anything he wanted, but the realistic side told her this was not possible and she was in for a long night.

Chapter Eight

"What the hell is that?"

Tara laughed at Kate's expression. "Well, that is our new dog, Daisy."

Kate sat her purse on the accent table inside the front door. She reached her hand out to the curious dog who had come over to sniff her.

"I'm pretty sure this is not the Daisy I remember," Kate exclaimed as she got multiple kisses from the new giant Daisy. "Are you guys seriously trying to pass this dog off as her old poodle?"

"No, this is Daisy Part Two." Tara led the way toward the rear of the house and into the kitchen. "And this is all Sam's idea. He really is trying, but some things are not working as well as others."

"And how is this working out with you and Sam?" Kate asked as she took a seat at the kitchen table.

Tara leaned against the countertop and gave a shrug. "We are taking it day by day, but as you can imagine this is difficult for everybody."

"Has Marley regained any memories?" Kate asked.

"Just that we were all supposed to go on a beach vacation, but that was planned right before Sam left. Unfortunately, that's the time frame where things get a little hazy with her memory."

Tara had already started looking for beach houses on the East Coast. She'd found several right on the beach, but most were either already rented or too pricey. She and Sam would have to discuss options. She didn't know what would be worse, the hours-long car ride with Sam or frolicking on the beach playing as a family.

"Wow," Kate gasped. "So you guys are going to take a real family vacation? Even with everything going on?"

Tara nodded and went to the refrigerator for a bottle of water. She handed one to her friend and took another for herself. She needed a distraction. The more she discussed this inevitable vacation, the more her nerves kicked into overdrive.

"That is what Marley wants," Tara stated. "We are doing anything we can to help her regain her memory. She's been home a few days and so far all she's recalled is that the original Daisy died. I'd like to get some sort of happy memories in her bank."

Kate rested one hand on her belly and clutched her water bottle with the other. "Is there anything I can do to help?"

"I don't even know what *I* can do to help." Being so confused and vulnerable was most infuriating. She wanted her daughter healed right this second. "I don't know what we're going to do when she regains her memories and realizes that Sam and I have split up. I'm so afraid she'll hate us for lying or she'll feel deceived, like she can't trust her own parents."

Kate offered a sympathetic smile. "She will see that her mom and dad came together to help her. She loves you both, so don't be so hard on yourself."

Tara prayed that her daughter would feel that way once all was said and done, and she regained control of her mind. Tara wasn't so sure a five-year-old could fully comprehend the sacrifices made by her parents.

"So, are you really keeping the massive dog?" Kate asked as Daisy came up beside her and took a seat.

Tara laughed and shook her head. "At this point, I don't have a choice. I'm outnumbered when it comes to the new Daisy. The slobber kind of grows on you, in a weird sort of way."

"I'll take your word for it," Kate stated as she patted Daisy's head. "Gray and I decided on baby names. Do you want to hear them?"

"Of course I do," Tara exclaimed. "It is killing me that I don't know if it is a boy or a girl. I guess I'll buy things for each and take back what you can't use. My credit card is so ready for a baby shopping spree."

Kate laughed and patted Tara's arm. "Calm down. We don't want our little one spoiled right off the bat."

"Fine." Tara pouted. "But I'm still going to spoil Baby Gallagher a little."

"Considering we're living over the bar, it's not like we're decorating the nursery pink or blue," Kate explained.

"Babies never know what their room looks like. Too many people get caught up in stuff that isn't important." Tara crossed to the kitchen table and took a seat. "The most important thing is love and security, and you and Gray will provide both. And the toys and fashionable clothes I'll provide."

Kate rolled her eyes and winced as her hand clutched the side of her belly.

"What is it?" Tara asked.

"Just Braxton Hicks," Kate hissed. "Damn things have been attacking out of nowhere."

Tara patted Kate's knee. "I remember those. You

only have about six weeks left. Everything will be worth it once you're holding your little bundle."

"That's what I hear, but I could do without these," Kate complained. "Sorry, I'm grouchy when I get a false contraction."

"Understandable. Nobody wants them until it's showtime," Tara joked.

Kate let out a long sigh and smiled. "There. It passed. So, where is Marley? I was hoping I would get to see her."

"Sam took her to visit his mother." There wasn't much else she could say and still be nice about the situation regarding her soon-to-be ex-mother-in-law. "We thought it was better that way instead of her coming to visit here."

"I don't understand that woman," Kate commented as Daisy rested her head on Kate's lap.

The sweet dog was apparently so happy to be free from the shelter, she loved on everyone. How could Tara say anything about drool puddles?

"Well, first she thought we married too fast," Tara explained, as if she could sum up her mother-in-law in only a few sentences. "She figured I was after a baby-daddy. Then, when I asked Sam to leave, she thought I was turning him away when he needed someone most."

Turning him away had been the toughest decision of her life. She'd heard the term *tough love* before, but she'd never had to implement it. Even now, she had layers of guilt recalling how ugly their words had been, how nasty their actions had gotten. Broken glass was nothing compared to shattered hearts.

Thankfully they'd kept Marley sheltered from the brunt of their falling out. Separating parents was never easy on a child, but they'd done all they could.

Well, Tara had done more because Sam had checked himself into rehab. But Tara had simply explained that Daddy was sick and had to go away to get better.

"Turning him away was the only way he was going to get the help he needed," Kate reminded her. "He still loves you, you know."

Tara chewed the inside of her lip to keep from admitting or denying any such thing. "We were married. I'm sure he still feels something for me."

No need to express he'd said as much two nights ago while he'd been holding her hand in bed.

Holding her hand. Like they hadn't made love in that exact spot, like he hadn't held her night after night in that very room. He'd simply held her hand and that simple touch had unlocked something in her heart that no kiss could have done.

There was a tenderness about Sam that reminded her of the man she'd married. But did that man even exist anymore? Every part of her wanted to believe so. But that was also a dangerous way of thinking.

"Sam stopped by the bar the other day."

Tara shifted her focus to Kate. "Is that right?"

She knew Sam always hung at the bar, mostly to visit Gray, and Gray would keep his eye on Sam. Over the past year, Gray had been a huge help in keeping Sam on the right path. Gray had been big brother, best friend, counselor...whatever Sam had needed.

Tara had kept her eye on him from a distance, praying and hoping he'd find his way. They'd kept their conversations cordial during drop off and pickup with the custody agreement. Sam had worked his ass off to crawl to the point he was at today and she was so proud of how far he'd come.

"He was there to see Gray, but he got me, instead," Kate stated with a smile and a shrug. "He's carrying quite a bit of emotion around."

Tara nodded, torn over how much to divulge, even to Kate. Everyone was invested in Sam and his recovery journey, but at the same time, Tara didn't want to say too much because her friends, Sam and even her own heart could take her words the wrong way.

The last thing she could afford was anyone thinking there was some happily-ever-after at the end of this. She knew her friends wanted the best for both her and Sam, but not everyone was meant for a happily-ever-after.

"He's carrying quite a bit," Tara agreed with a

slow nod. "He told me he took indefinite time off to be with Marley and me. I worry with this new job that maybe he should go in so he doesn't lose it."

"He'd do anything for you guys. There's no job that compares to his family."

That familiar prick of burn to her eyes and clogged throat had Tara coming to her feet and crossing to the door. "Well," she said as she cleared her throat. "Tell me those baby names."

Kate slid her hand over Daisy's head and stroked her ears. "Obviously you and Sam are off the topic table, so I'll give in and tell you."

Tara opened the screen door and waved her hand. "Come on, Daisy. Let's go."

"Oh, you don't have to send her out on my account," Kate declared.

Daisy galloped out the door, nearly knocking Tara over in the process. The poor thing had a tendency toward the clumsy side.

"She hadn't been out in a while and she needs to run around the fenced-in yard to work off some energy...and to dispose of that slobber outside." Tara took a seat at the table. "Now, tell me the names. Wait, did you already tell Lucy?"

Kate shook her head. "Not yet, so don't say anything."

Tara patted the table. "Out with it."

"Well, if we have a boy, we're naming him Liam Gray Gallagher to carry on with Gray's Irish heritage, and if we have a girl, we're naming her Fallon Katherine Gallagher."

Well, there went those tears she'd been trying to keep under control. "Those are beautiful. I can't believe we're going to have a little one in less than two months."

"Might as well be forever," Kate said on an exasperated sigh. "I feel like my skin cannot possibly stretch any more."

"Oh, it can and it will." Tara laughed.

Kate cringed. "Don't tell me that. I'm in denial and I know that my waist will never be the same."

"You'll bounce right back," Tara assured her. "But no matter what you look like, having a baby is life changing and the most rewarding, stressful, important job ever. It's seriously all emotions wrapped into one little being that you created."

Kate smiled and rubbed her belly. "I can't wait. Gray has spurts of overprotectiveness, which can be sweet but annoying and then he relaxes. But then he reads something else online and worries again, so the cycle starts all over."

Tara had a pang of longing. She'd been alone when she'd been expecting Marley. Her jerk of an ex had abandoned her at the mere mention of pregnancy and she hadn't met Sam until Marley was around two. She couldn't help but wonder what Sam would've been like as an expectant father. Definitely attentive, most likely overbearing and hovering.

"What's that smile?" Kate asked.

Tara blinked away the mental image and shook her head. "Just thinking of you and Gray as parents. You're going to be amazing."

Daisy barked outside as car doors slammed. Marley stormed in the back door and ran through the house and up the stairs. The resounding slam of her bedroom door echoed into the kitchen.

Kate glanced to Tara. "What happened?"

Sam stepped in the door and Tara came to her feet. "Sam?"

"She had a memory."

Chapter Nine

"You never should have brought that damn dog here."

Tara paced across the living room. Sam merely stood at the base of the steps, his arm over the banister, and remained quiet.

Couldn't he say something? Anything? She wasn't sure if she was gearing up for a fight to get out her frustrations or if she wanted him to agree with her. Mercy, she was a mess. She didn't even recognize herself lately.

Sam's silence grated on her very last nerve. How could he be so calm when Marley was upstairs crying over the memory of losing her dog? Well, she'd already had that memory, but now she recalled how her beloved pet had passed and had relived the moment all over again.

Precisely what Tara had feared would happen all along…and not just with Marley's pet. All of this was going to get worse before it got better. When Marley regained all of her thoughts, she would learn they had been lying to her.

"I brought the dog to help our daughter heal," Sam said in that calm voice of his. He'd always been so in control…until that point when he wasn't. "I know it was a rash decision, but at the time I would've done anything to see her smile."

Tara stopped pacing and stared across the room at him. His eyes settled onto hers, holding her in place. He'd always managed to do that. He could stop her with one look, one crooked grin that would send her heart beating even faster.

"I've yet to see what would make you smile again."

His words hit her hard, but she did not have the time or the mental stamina to analyze what he meant for the impact they had on her heart or the future.

"This is not about me," Tara exclaimed, trying to stay focused on the real problem. "What did you say to her when she remembered how Daisy died?"

Kate had left once she discovered there was a serious problem. Tara had promised to call her later and fill her in. Now Tara was still waiting for Sam to explain what had actually happened while they were at his mother's house.

"We were on our way home when a dog ran out in front of the car." Sam stepped away from the staircase and shoved his hands in his pockets. "I slammed on my brakes and the dog continued to run across the street to the other side. Marley started crying and said she remembered Daisy getting hit by a car. I tried to explain that the doctor said because of the bump on her head some memories were missing and would likely come back in pieces. I really did not know what to say, so I tried to console her."

Tara knew he'd probably done all he could. Still, she wanted to place the blame somewhere for her daughter's upset. But how could she target Sam when this entire chaotic mess was due to an accident?

Taking her hair behind her ears, Tara blew out a sigh. "I'm going to go upstairs and talk to her."

"I'll go with you."

Tara held up her hand and shook her head. "Let me handle this."

The muscles in Sam's jaw ticked, but he ultimately nodded his head in agreement. She wasn't trying to push him away—well, maybe she was. All of their emotions were running on high alert right now, and she wanted to console her daughter alone. Who knew what he'd promise Marley in an attempt to get her to smile again? Likely she really would end up with that iguana.

Tara started for the steps, but Sam's hand reached out, his fingers curling around her arm. The rough pad of his thumb gently stroked over her bare, sensitive skin, causing way too many emotions and way too many tingles for her comfort.

"I know you keep wanting to do this alone, but I'm not going anywhere until she is better." He leaned closer to her ear and whispered, "And until you see that I've changed."

Tara did not look at him. She knew if she turned her head their lips would brush and she simply could not afford that—not when she was still feeling their kiss from that first night.

He slowly released her, and Tara headed up the steps to her daughter's bedroom. She eased open the door and found Marley sitting on her bed hugging her stuffed mermaid.

Without a word, Tara sat on the edge of the bed and placed her hand on her daughter's leg. "I'm sorry you remembered seeing Daisy hurt."

Marley sniffed and continued to toy with the yarn hair on the mermaid. Like most children, Marley closed in on herself when she was hurting. Likely because she didn't know how to express her emotions properly or she just didn't want to. Tara needed her daughter to know she wasn't alone.

"Your daddy said he told you about the bump

on your head making some of your memories go away."

Marley nodded. "Why can't you guys just tell me everything?"

"Well, the doctor thought it was best if you remembered on your own."

Tara couldn't say too much else without giving it all away, but having her daughter relive all the terrible moments over the past year was going to be heart-wrenching. Perhaps she would remember some of the good memories, as well, and those would outweigh the bad.

But Tara doubted it. Between Sam leaving, the ruined family vacations and Daisy dying, the past year had actually been pure hell for all of them. At this point Tara only hoped she could make happy, new memories and keep Marley's spirits up.

"Will I get to keep the new Daisy?"

Tara smiled and patted Marley's leg. "Of course you can."

Over the past few days Tara had gotten used to the slobbering, the flying fur and constantly walking around a giant beast in her home. How could she not love the new Daisy? The beast was a cuddly ball and so affectionate.

Marley sat up, tossed her mermaid aside and threw her arms around Tara's neck. Tara hugged her daughter and squeezed her tight. This was only one hurdle of many they still had to overcome, and there was no way of knowing how everything else would turn out once Marley discovered the whole truth.

"I'm going to go make us some lunch," Tara stated. "Why don't you go outside and play with Daisy, because she has missed you."

Marley hopped off her bed and raced from the room. Tara figured that had gone much better than she'd originally thought. Then again, children were resilient and Marley hadn't recalled all the issues from her missing year.

On a sigh, Tara came to her feet and went into her bedroom. She needed to change her shirt since she had dog hair all over it. She was still getting used to changing her clothes before cooking because she really didn't want to serve up a side of St. Bernard fur.

As soon as she opened her closet, Tara stilled at the envelope hanging from a bright yellow ribbon around one hanger.

Another letter. She knew full well what this was before she even reached for it. This was a note with Sam's feelings.

Before she and Sam were married, during their marriage and since he'd been out of rehab, he would randomly leave her notes. Sometimes they were lengthy and heartfelt; other times they were short, sweet, and utterly heart-melting...sometimes panty-melting.

No matter the highs or lows of their lives, this

one constant had always remained. Persistence had been one of the many reasons she'd fallen in love with Sam. He never gave up and the one time she'd needed him to, he refused.

Sam knew exactly what to do, what to say, to get her emotions open and vulnerable. Even now, especially now.

But she couldn't let him back in. She simply couldn't, for both of their sakes.

Pulling up her courage and strength, Tara reached for the ribbon and slid the silk strands loose from the hanger. She glanced over her shoulder to make sure she was still alone. Sam had to have placed this in here after she'd dressed this morning and before he went to his mother's house.

Tara took the envelope and went over to sit on the edge of her bed. She didn't know why this one made her so nervous when the others hadn't. Perhaps it was because he was in her house now; he was actually right downstairs, likely waiting for her reaction.

With shaky fingers, Tara opened the envelope and pulled out the folded sheet of paper. In his familiar slanted handwriting, she read the simple words, "I'm not perfect, but I'm better than I was. I'm always here for you."

For as determined and persistent as Sam was, he was also uncomplicated. Those words summed up his essential being.

She knew he wanted to help and be their supportive rock. There was no doubting the love he had for Marley. He'd always treated her as his own because in Sam's world she was his.

But part of Tara couldn't help but worry that when things got too tough or things did not resolve quickly enough with Marley, would he head to the pills? Would he be able to handle life's obstacles all on his own and not revert to the old Sam? That addiction might have started from an accident and a simple prescription, but he'd turned to them later when he just couldn't cope.

That was one risk she couldn't take. Not for Marley, not for herself and mostly not for the man she still loved with her whole heart. She had to keep him pushing forward and the only way she knew how was to keep him at a distance.

Tara folded the letter neatly and put it into the envelope. She crossed to her dresser and opened the top drawer, laying the envelope with the stack of the others.

Despite what happened between them, she had kept every single letter he ever wrote to her. Call her sentimental, or perhaps just someone wanting to hold on to the one perfect thing about their relationship, but she needed those letters. It was the only way she remained connected to him emotionally without anyone truly knowing how she felt.

Tara went to her closet to grab a different shirt

and quickly changed before heading downstairs. Squeals of laughter came from the backyard and Tara glanced out to see Sam and Marley being chased by Daisy. An instant flash of when Sam had first come into their lives slid into her mind. Marley had instantly taken to Sam and he to her. They had a stronger bond than most blood relatives and their little family had been picture-perfect. She'd never imagined anything could rip them apart.

Swallowing the lump in her throat, Tara shifted her focus from the scene outside and started preparing lunch. All of this time she had been worried about how Sam would deal with the situation of living here again, but what she really needed to worry about was herself. Letting go of the pain would be too easy, but she could not do that again. She would always love him, but she'd learned a tough life lesson that you can still love someone and have to set them free.

She just wished it didn't hurt so damn bad.

He wasn't sure if he was an utter fool or if this was a brilliant plan. Possibly a healthy dose of both, but what did he have to lose?

Sam stood outside of Marley's bedroom door as Tara started tucking her in for the night. He missed these days. Even though his time here was temporary, he was glad he was here for the nightly regime where he'd come in and kiss his daughter good-night.

Though he'd never quite done anything like what was about to happen.

Sam glanced at himself, thankful that nobody else could see him at the moment. Gray and Noah would never have let him live this down. Hell, any man he'd ever known wouldn't have let him forget his state of dress.

But there wasn't anything he wouldn't do for his family and acting like a fool fell right into that category.

He eased the door open and cleared his throat to get the attention of his girls. Tara glanced up, her mouth dropping open, her eyes wide. Marley had the exact reaction he was hoping for. She burst into laughter and rolled on her bed, kicking her feet.

"Well, those are different pajamas," Tara said with a wide smile on her face and a gleam in her eye he hadn't seen in far too long. "Is this something new you're trying?"

That smile was like a punch to his gut. "You don't like my coconut bra and grass skirt?"

"I love it, Daddy," Marley squealed as she hopped off her bed. She wrapped her arms around him and Sam hugged her as he met Tara's questioning gaze.

"I figured this was the best way to tell you I booked our beach trip." Sam patted Marley and smoothed her hair beneath his palm. "Well, I could've told you, but I figured this was better."

"I don't even want to know where you got it," Tara muttered, shaking her head. She came to her feet and tucked her hair behind her ears. "I was looking into something similar. But I admit I never would've thought to announce it this way."

Sam didn't know if he could've handled Tara in a coconut bra and grass skirt, so perhaps that was a good thing.

"I'd say this family deserves a vacation, don't you?" he asked. "I think lounging on the beach is exactly the break we need."

Tara's eyes raked over his bare chest and Sam would have been lying if he didn't admit that he loved every single visual lick. He'd thought Tara would never look at him that way again, and he sure as hell never thought it would be while he was wearing a coconut bra and a grass skirt. Marley jumped up and down with her hands extended high and Sam lifted her into his arms.

"When are we going, Daddy? When?"

He squeezed his girl tight and laughed. "My boss has a beach house in South Carolina he is going to let us rent. It's secluded, with its own private beach, and the home is fully stocked. We were discussing vacations and when I mentioned I was looking for a house, he told me about this. He said there was a cancellation at the last minute and, lucky for us, we get the place for four whole days. We can leave the day after tomorrow."

"Two days?" Tara repeated. "That doesn't give us much time to plan."

"And Mommy promised me we could find a new bathing suit," Marley added. "I want a purple one."

He sat her on the floor and tapped the end of her nose. "Then I guess we better get shopping."

Sam was not letting this opportunity pass him by. The opening had presented itself and he was taking his family on the promised vacation…though a year late. Even though Tara remained across the room she continued to stare at him with wide, wondering eyes.

"Maybe we should wait a little bit," Tara stated as she continued to stare at him. "I mean, we do have a lot going on."

Sam was not going to let her back out of this. He had vowed to be there for his family and he was going to start by making good on all of the promises he had broken. He refused to let them down again, no matter how minor the situation was.

"But, Mommy, I really want to go now," Marley said as she wiggled out of Sam's arms. "Can we please go in two days? Please, please? You don't even have to get me a new suit."

Tara sank onto the edge of the bed to be eye level with Marley. "We will go. We all could use a getaway."

"I hope you don't mind if I take this for my new suit," Sam stated as he pointed at his dollar-store ensemble.

Marley giggled and shook her head. "I don't think so, Daddy. Maybe you should take your swim trunks."

Sam reached behind his neck and pulled the string, then untied the string behind his back. He tossed the coconut bra onto Marley's bed.

"I suppose you're right," Sam stated. "I can take you shopping tomorrow if you want to find a new suit."

Marley's eyes widened. "You will take me shopping?"

Sam shrugged "Sure. I'd love to buy my favorite girl new things for our vacation."

Before he could say anything else, Tara came to her feet, holding the comforter up and gesturing for Marley to get under the covers.

"It's time for bed," Tara said as she tucked Marley in. "We can talk vacation tomorrow."

Tara kissed Marley on the head and turned to face Sam. Was it his imagination or had her eyes narrowed? He couldn't tell if she was turned on or angry. Perhaps a good mixture of both.

"Good night, baby." Sam moved forward and kissed her on the forehead. "Sweet dreams."

He turned off her bedside light and walked out of the room, easing the door shut behind him. When he shifted, the edge of the grass skirt tickled his knees so he reached around the back and jerked the knot on the skirt.

Fisting it, he went into his bedroom, where Tara stood with her arms crossed, lips thin, shoulders squared. Clearly ready for a fight. And here all he'd come to battle with was a plastic costume.

"Something you want to say?" he asked as he tossed the skirt onto the floor.

Once again, her eyes raked over him as he stood before her wearing a pair of running shorts. If she kept looking at him like that, he was going to start to believe there might be a chance for them. He had never stopped wanting his old life back. Even those nights he had spent in rehab alone, shaking and afraid, he'd held on to the memories of his family and the love they'd created. He had wanted Tara, had needed her, but he'd been of no use to her at that point.

Now he was a new man, but with realistic expectations of life. He knew anything they'd had was gone. But did that mean they couldn't start over? Was that even an inkling in her mind?

"You can't keep doing this."

Confused, Sam crossed his arms over his chest and shook his head. "You'll have to clarify."

She waved a hand toward him. "All of that," she stated, as if her vague explanation made this any clearer.

"You'll have to be more specific."

Tara growled, threw her arms in the air and headed toward her dresser. "Everything. The new dog, the continuous letters, the damn coconut bra and all this charm. Just stop."

He watched as she opened her drawer and pulled out the stack of envelopes. There was no way to suppress the smile, and he didn't even try. He had given up all hope of basically anything between them ever again. Well, other than sharing custody of Marley.

What did it mean that she had kept every single letter he had written? From her frustrated tone, he had to believe she still cared more than she wanted to admit.

Tara tossed the letters onto the bed with dramatic flair and turned her focus to him with narrowed eyes and tight lips. Who was she angrier at, him for sending his thoughts through handwritten notes or herself for holding on to each one?

"You can't keep doing this to me," Tara cried, frustration lacing her tone. "I can't ride this roller coaster of emotions with you, with Marley, with everything. You are making this difficult by making me remember exactly what I lost."

The joy he had felt moments ago simply vanished at her last statement that came out on a broken sob. Sam had no right, but that did not stop him from crossing the room and taking her in his arms.

She stiffened against him, but he held tighter. He held on to her as if he could take the hurt away, as if holding their bodies together would somehow make this better. He would do anything to ease her pain but he had no clue how. Being helpless had never sat well with him, and he'd damn well try to make her happy again because sitting back and doing nothing sure as hell wasn't an option.

As if she'd run out of energy fighting herself, fighting him, Tara dropped her head to his chest. An instant later her body trembled, but Sam realized she was trying to keep her crying hidden from him. Again, he had no right to think he should be offering comfort when he'd caused the damage, but he kissed the top of her head and refused to let go.

Moving his hand over her spine, Sam murmured, "Let it out. Don't keep trying to be strong. There's nobody here but us."

She tipped her head back and stared at him with unshed tears shimmering in her bright eyes. "Don't you understand? I can't just let go. I'm afraid if I let go, I will never be whole again."

Sam looked into those bright blue eyes swimming with tears, wondering how many nights she had struggled with this control, trying to remain strong for everyone around her. Had she turned to anybody for comfort? He wanted to be that person, but there was no way she would let him and he had no place asking.

His eyes darted to the letters strewn across the bed merely feet away. Maybe she hated him for what he'd done, and that was nothing less than he deserved, but those letters spoke volumes about what was truly hidden inside her heart.

She blinked and one lone tear slid down her creamy cheek. That absolutely gutted him. Sam framed her face with his hands and swiped at the moisture with the pad of his thumb. She continued to stare at him as if searching for answers, but he didn't have any. All he had were these feelings, too many feelings that he had tried to suppress over the past year. There was only so much a man could take.

And holding his wife as she cried over his actions was more than he could handle.

Sam stepped into her until their bodies aligned fully and he slid his lips over hers ever so gently. He kept his eyes open as her lids fluttered. She was just as affected as he was and they were both an emotional mess. Clearly this was not their smartest move.

"This is a bad idea," she whispered, voicing his thoughts.

"I'm consoling my wife."

"You keep calling me that like we have a future."

Sam knew they didn't have a chance, but they did have right now. He parted his lips over hers and threaded his fingers through her hair, arching her back so he could take what he wanted—something he sure as hell didn't deserve.

When she slid her delicate arms around his waist, her fingers gliding over his bare skin, it was all Sam could do not to turn her and put her on the bed and take every single thing he had been aching for this past year.

He had missed her touch, had missed everything, really. Tara opened her mouth beneath his, not only accepting his kiss but returning it with a need all her own. He knew she was using him as an outlet for her feelings, but he didn't give a damn. Maybe they were using each other at this moment. And he was going to take what he could and ignore every red flag waving around in his head—and damn all consequences that would follow.

Sam shifted to change the angle of the kiss. There was a hunger inside him that had been reawakened by her simple touch. Her melting against him gave Sam the green light he'd been waiting for.

Now he spun her around until the backs of her legs hit the edge of the bed. When she tumbled over, he went with her, never removing his lips from hers. She spread her legs so he settled evenly between her thighs. She thrust her hands through his hair, her kiss urgent, her body arching against his.

Sam's hand went between their bodies as he pulled back slightly. He needed to touch her even more than he already was. He trailed his fingers up her bare leg and kept his eyes on her. Any sign of hesitation and he would stop.

Sam knew if this went too far she would have regrets. And as much as he wanted her, all of her, he would not leave her feeling even more lost on the other side of their intimacy. He had made a vow to himself that everything would be about her and Marley from the moment he became sober and into their future. Whatever the future may be.

He slid his finger beneath the edge of her panties. Her eyes widened as her fingertips dug into his forearms. Her breath came in soft pants…the same pants he'd fantasized about for so long.

As he stroked his fingertips over her sensitive area, Tara's lids fluttered once again as she bit her lip and arched upward. This was everything he had missed, watching her come undone and knowing he was the one pleasuring her.

The moment he slid his finger into her she cried out, but he covered her lips with his. He couldn't seem to touch her enough, yet he needed to go slow and he needed to make sure she knew this was all for her. She lifted her hips against his hand and he let her set the rhythm. No matter what she wanted, he was sure as hell going to be the one to give it to her.

Maybe that was too primal, perhaps he had no right, but he was human and this was his wife. His wife. How could he ever let her go? Even though this moment would be fleeting, for the first time in a long time there was a blossom of hope deep within him. But he could not get too hung up on that—he would only end up hurting himself once again. And those selfish thoughts would not keep him on track to make Tara's life easier.

When Tara's hips jerked harder, Sam watched her complete and utter control snap as pleasure consumed her. She broke from his lips and squeezed her eyes shut. Sam knew this moment would be forever in his memory bank. There was nothing sexier than his wife when she let passion consume her.

Then her body slowed, the trembling eased.

Sam knew the moment she had slipped into reality. Her eyes flew open, the grip on his arm loosened and her entire body went lax beneath him. Sam eased his hand from between her legs and smoothed her nightgown over her thighs. He had to steel his heart against whatever she decided to say or do from this moment on. He came to his feet but remained at the edge of the bed staring at her.

"Sam."

"Don't say anything." He couldn't bear to hear the words that would come from her mouth. He already saw regret in her eyes. "I know what this is and what this isn't. You needed a release and I selfishly ached to give it to you."

He went to the dresser and pulled out a gray T-shirt then slid it over his head. When he turned to face her, an onslaught of emotions nearly brought him to his knees. There she sat in the middle of the bed, lying on the letters he had written her, each one from his heart. Each one from a moment in his life he'd wanted to reach out to her in person.

When he'd laid her on the bed he'd been so intent on her needs he'd forgotten them. There'd been too much to take in with the sight of her lying there—too much that he was afraid to analyze.

"I'll be on the couch tonight," he told her. "It's not a good idea for me to sleep beside you right now."

Before she could say anything else, Sam walked out of the room. They both needed space after what had just happened. Emotions had been running high before this, and now he had crossed some invisible line and he had no clue what territory they were in anymore. Sam knew he was making things more difficult for both of them, but damn it, he was human and now that he had sampled his wife again, he was more than ready to fight for his family.

Chapter Ten

Marley burst into the beach house and ran from room to room. Tara sat her suitcase down, but the moment Daisy came barreling through, she ran into it and knocked the case to the floor with a loud thud. Not to mention she was leaving a trail of drool droplets on the glossy hardwood floors.

Fabulous. They'd been inside all of ten seconds and already left their mark.

Sam sat the rest of the luggage on the floor and bent to right hers. He swiped his hand on his shorts and let out a sigh.

"It was a mistake to bring that mammoth," Tara stated as she took in her surroundings. This place screamed money, from the classy white oversized sofas to the artwork on the walls. "I can't even imagine the damage she's going to do and we'll have to pay for. Starting with getting all the floors cleaned."

Sam laughed and a familiar tingle washed over her. For the past two days they'd done well to dodge each other. Though, even with avoiding him altogether or having Marley as a buffer in the same room, nothing seemed to squelch Tara's desire. Sam had selflessly given her pleasure and then walked away as if he hadn't wanted to take things further.

That thought alone had kept her up the past two nights. What game was he playing? Was he purposely trying to confuse her even more? Or did he truly believe they had a chance at a future?

"I assure you that Daisy is welcome here," Sam stated. "Bill is a huge animal lover and brings his own pets when he comes. I already covered this with him and he's fully aware of Daisy's issues."

"He brings his own pets?" Tara repeated. "Now Daisy will pee everywhere to mark her territory."

"Stop worrying." Sam came to stand in front of her and looked her straight in the eye. "Bill has a cleaning service that comes in between guests. All signs of Daisy will be gone. Your only job now is to relax."

Relax? With him standing this close? With those memories of the way he'd touched her, the way he'd pleasured her, so vivid in her mind? Not likely.

And then there was that damn tattoo he had. She'd wanted to ask him multiple times about it, but it never seemed right.

"This place is so cool," Marley squealed as she came from the hallway. "Can I put my suit on and we can go to the beach? Please? Oh, Daisy said she wants to come, too."

Tara shook her head, more from exhaustion than anything. The car ride hadn't been nearly as bad as she'd feared. Being in a confined space with Sam was fine considering a giant St. Bernard head had settled between the front seats for most of the seven-hour drive.

The twinkle in Marley's eyes and her clasped hands had Tara nodding. "I suppose having her outside means less time she has to be in here tearing things up that aren't mine or leaving permanent watermarks on the floor."

"You're not relaxing," Sam warned with a low growl. "Go get your suit on."

His eyes held hers and she shivered. Had his voice dropped even lower into sultry, sexy territory? Maybe the beach wasn't the best idea. Even though Marley was with them, that wouldn't erase the fact Tara and Sam would be half-dressed for most of this trip and the beach area was private with this luxury home.

"Thanks, Dad."

Marley raced off and Daisy scampered after her,

sliding as she tried to get traction on the hardwood floors.

"I could stay here and unpack," Tara suggested, instantly realizing she sounded desperate to be alone.

Sam propped his hands on his hips and raised his brows. "We're only here a few days. I think we'll be fine digging out of the suitcases."

He took a step closer and smiled the signature grin that assaulted every single nerve in only the most delicious of ways. "Unless you're afraid you won't be able to resist staring at my bare chest."

The way he delivered the words was completely joking, but in all honesty—at least to herself—that's precisely what she was afraid of. For the past two nights, Sam had slept on the sofa and woken before Marley got up so as not to raise too many questions. Thankfully their daughter still had no idea their marriage was a complete farce.

But having Sam so near, having him reawaken suppressed feelings, was dangerously close to teetering over the line of the real thing.

Tara figured anything she said now would only give away her temporary feelings so she skirted around Sam and grabbed the handle of her suitcase. She wheeled it down the hall and found the master suite—which opened with wide double doors.

Talk about a luxury beach house. The second

the doors opened, she had a sweeping view of the ocean.

Tara crossed the room, forgetting her suitcase. The breathtaking sight beckoned her to get a closer look.

She curled her fingers around the handles, and pushing the patio doors wide, she stepped onto the private balcony. The onslaught of sea mist hit her and she raised her face to the sun, welcoming the warmth and fresh air. She loved the mountains of Tennessee, but there was something so crisp and invigorating about a saltwater wind.

Maybe this trip was exactly what she needed, what they all needed. How could anyone be in a bad mood or worry with all of this beauty and serenity? The privacy certainly helped because they could focus on Marley with no outside noise. Even if the getaway was only four days, this was still the vacation Sam had promised Marley.

And slowly she realized he was making good on all of those old promises.

"I've never seen a more beautiful sight."

Tara's heart clenched at Sam's sultry voice. She glanced over her shoulder, discovering he wasn't too far away, but his eyes were locked on hers… not the magnificent horizon.

All air caught in her lungs and she shifted her focus to the view before he could read anything in her eyes.

"Yes, well, I hope you make sure Bill knows how much we appreciate staying here." She gripped the railing even tighter to get a grasp on reality. This was all temporary…the vacation and the man. "And no more charming comments."

"Am I not to compliment my wife?"

"You really need to quit calling me that," Tara stated as she forced herself not to turn around. "You even said the other night you knew there was no future."

"Oh, yes, the other night." Sam came to stand beside her, but he turned and rested against the railing. "I've been waiting on you to bring that up. For now, you are my wife, no matter how short-term or the fact that we are pretending to be happy. Even you cannot escape this."

Tara pulled in a shaky breath. "The sooner you can sign those papers, the better off we will both be."

She knew the words were harsh, but somebody had to be realistic. Had he signed those papers when he received them, this would be so much easier on her sanity. They would still have had to play the roles of a happily married couple for Marley, but at least they would both know the end had already come.

Where things stood now was too confusing, too painful.

"Maybe I'm not ready to give up," Sam stated,

the soft words washing over her like the sea breeze. But the impact hit her hard, nearly taking the breath from her lungs.

Tara blinked against the burn in her eyes and vainly attempted to blame it on the wind. In the days since Marley's accident, he'd left her with the obvious notion that he was fighting for his family.

"Sex will not fix our problems." She turned to face him, trying to focus on keeping her heart somewhat intact. "Can we please call a truce for the duration of our vacation? I can't have you doing any more charming things, giving me lengthy glances or saying anything that will make me remember how things used to be."

He stared at her for a moment, the muscles in his jaw clenching, before he finally nodded in agreement. "You have my word."

He pushed off the railing and went into the bedroom. There was a subtle sound of the zipper on his suitcase, followed by rustling. Tara remained outside to gather her composure.

When she spun around, once again her lungs seized up and her heart clenched.

Was this how she'd be living her life so long as she had to fake this marriage? Each time she got a glimpse of Sam, would she continue to have that hitch of emotions?

He wasn't even looking in her direction. In fact, his back was to her. But seeing him all muscular in those swim trunks was flat-out playing dirty. Damn that man, he probably didn't even realize what he was doing. Oh, she fully believed he would use every weapon in his arsenal because he had conceded too easily on the balcony. But right at this moment she knew he was getting ready to take their daughter to the beach.

He shifted slightly and she caught another glimpse of the tattoo. Before she could fully process the image, he headed out of the room.

Tara grabbed her own suitcase and sat it on the trunk at the end of the bed. She unzipped the case and flipped the top up to find her one-piece suit. She hadn't been brave enough to pack that blue bikini Sam had loved on her. She needed every ounce of material covering her during this vacation. Because there was no way around it. Someone was going to get hurt when Marley's memory returned and this charade was up.

Chapter Eleven

"No, Daisy!"

Sam laughed as Daisy plowed through the sandcastle he and Marley had just finished. Sam didn't know who was having more fun, the dog or his daughter. They had been out most of the evening and the sun was starting to set. If he could wrap this day in a box and keep it forever, he would.

Seeing his daughter play made him smile and lifted his heart in a way therapy never could. Spending time with his family again, with everything he had missed and everything he thought he had lost, was the blossom of hope he so desperately needed. Maybe he hadn't screwed things up beyond repair.

Maybe he could find a way to start over and create an even better life.

Because he had lost it all. He'd lost every ounce of this happiness, and maybe this was but a fleeting moment. That didn't mean he couldn't try, couldn't fight for what he'd let slip from his grasp. He wasn't even sure he deserved this moment, but he wasn't going to turn it away or sulk over the past. All he could do was control the present and build for the future.

Sam vowed to enjoy these days with his family and he would let fate take care of itself later. Marley might be missing a year of her memories, but he was determined to give her new memories to override the bad.

"I'm going to head to the house to start dinner," Tara stated as she pulled on her cover-up.

That flimsy, sheer white material did nothing to hide the curves of her body and her black one-piece swimsuit. She could try to shield herself all she wanted, but he knew every square inch of her body, and nothing could erase that image burned in his mind.

Sam slid his fingertips against his palms, recalling exactly how she'd felt in his arms the other night. He wanted to touch her again, to pleasure her, but he'd promised not to make things more difficult. He was a patient man. All he could do was show her how much he still loved her, how much he had changed.

"I'll go start dinner," Sam said as he came to his feet. "You guys stay here and play."

"Are you sure?" Tara asked.

Sam picked up his towel and looped it around his neck. "Positive. I need to return a call for work and I have something special I wanted to make tonight."

He turned on his heel and headed toward the house, leaving Tara staring at him with her mouth wide.

Good. He wanted to keep her on her toes, keep her wondering what he would do next. Because she was going to learn there wasn't anything he wouldn't do for them. He knew she had had a less than stellar upbringing and unstable parents, so his betrayal and abandonment had only added to that wariness. All he could do at this point was to make their lives better any way he knew how.

And if wearing a coconut bra made his girls laugh again, then bring on the ridiculous costume. He was comfortable enough in his masculinity to pull that outfit off…so long as he was in the privacy of his own home.

Once Sam got inside, he quickly showered and grabbed his cell phone, which he'd left charging on the nightstand in the bedroom.

With the phone in hand, he stared at the bed. Sam's gut tightened at the thought of lying next to his wife once again. The other night when he'd reached for her hand, it had shifted something inside him, something he'd missed and wanted back with every bit of his soul.

But right now he had other things to deal with and tonight's problems would come soon enough.

Sam quickly dialed his boss and headed toward the kitchen to start dinner. This was definitely like old times. When Tara would have clients running late or last-minute emergencies at the office, he'd cooked dinner. He'd actually loved that part of their marriage. Taking care of her had been his greatest joy…until it wasn't.

"Hey, Sam," Bill answered on the second ring, pulling Sam from his thoughts.

He stood at the kitchen sink and glanced out onto the beach where Daisy was still running like a mad bull and his wife and daughter were attempting to build yet another sandcastle.

"Hey, man. I'm just returning your call. First, let me say how much I appreciate you letting us use your house."

"It's no problem at all. Have you guys settled in well?"

Sam searched through the cabinets until he came up with the pans he'd need. "We did. Marley and Tara are building sandcastles and having a blast."

"Has Marley recovered any memories?"

Sam tried his best to push aside the disappointment. He and Tara had discussed how little Marley had remembered, considering the accident had been over a week ago.

Still, as her father, as a man in general, he always had the need to fix everything right now—especially where his family was concerned. So this sitting around and waiting was pure hell. He wasn't sure what he'd expected as far as a time frame for Marley's memories to return went, but that didn't stop him from wishing for an instant miracle. He hated that his daughter was a prisoner in her own mind and there wasn't a damn thing he could do to help her.

"No, she hasn't."

"I'm sorry to hear that," his boss said, compassion flooding his voice. "It will happen. She's a strong little girl with strong-willed parents."

Sam nodded, even though his boss couldn't see him. "I assume you are calling about the Murray project."

"I really hated to bother you on vacation, but seeing as how you were the head of this new construction build, I wanted to run a few things by you so that way when you came in you weren't in the dark and didn't feel like we did things without your permission. It's regarding a redesign."

The only man to give Sam a second chance at a career Sam loved was on the other end of this call. So, if Bill was calling and asking for extra work,

Sam sure as hell was going to deliver on every single thing his boss asked. And he was going to go above and beyond because this would be the best design he'd ever come up with.

Sam smiled as he turned away from the window and headed to the pantry. "I work for you, remember? This is your company."

"That may be, but you owned a company that was a huge success and I'm damn lucky you came to work for me. So I figure treating you like an equal is the best way to get you to stay here."

Sam chuckled as he pulled out a box of pasta. "Considering I need this job and you saved my ass, I'm certainly not going anywhere. So what's up with the project? Wait, you said redesign." Sam set the box of pasta on the island and gripped the phone. "Murray changed his mind again, didn't he?"

"Afraid so," Bill stated with a weary tone. "He has decided to expand his initial building and wants to know how we can add an extra twelve hundred square feet."

The blueprints of the new country club in Stonerock ran through Sam's head. The idea of having to start over on this project made him cringe, but at the same time this was job security and Sam would do whatever it took to please the client.

Besides, this was also one of the best forms of therapy for him—using his mind to create something, then building it from scratch. The process was always grueling and time-consuming, but he wouldn't change it for anything because the end result was always rewarding.

"I'll get right on it," Sam promised.

"I hesitated to call, but I figured you would want to be the man in charge."

Sam couldn't help but feel a surge of pride at the confidence his boss had in him. Not long ago Sam had his own construction outfit, but of course that was another thing he'd ruined on his long path of destruction. The pills had hindered his mind on days and there had been projects he'd fallen behind on, others he'd forgotten completely. The snowball effect kept going until he'd hit the bottom.

Addiction stretched wide and enveloped so many people in its nasty web of lies, deceit and heartache. When he had gotten out of rehab and was trying to piece his life back together, Bill had been the only one who had seen the potential in Sam...the potential to regain the life he'd once had.

So Sam was sure as hell going to do everything he could to make Bill proud and pleased that he had hired him. If that meant working extra hours on vacation, then so be it. Because everything intertwined together...his work spilled over into his family and vice versa.

So when he was successful in one, he would certainly be successful in the other.

"How soon does he want to see the new plans?" Sam asked.

"Believe it or not, he is flexible on that. He wants the design to be perfect before we proceed. But I would like to give him something within the next two weeks if possible."

Sam was already configuring the new layout and calculating how long it would take him to come up with something to show.

"Can you send me more specifics on what he wants the new space for and if he has any particular dimensions? Will this area need a door, windows? Why am I telling you this? You know what to send me."

"I do." Bill let out a chuckle. "And I'll get right on the specs and get those to you. I wanted to talk to you over the phone instead of emailing to make sure you were on board. I didn't want this to be too much on your plate."

The front door to the beach house opened and closed followed by the giggling laughter of his daughter sliding on the floor with her new dog. The sounds were literally music to his ears.

A thick burn welled up in his throat as he heard those little noises that had once meant everything to him. There were so many things he'd taken for granted with his family, and every part of him wanted that life back. Not what he'd had…but something even better because he knew the potential was there.

Which meant he was going to have to work hard to provide for his family and show them he was a new man.

"Yes, I can have that done within two weeks."

Tara came to stand on the other side of the island. She had pulled her hair up to stop it from blowing in the wind but the shorter back half had already fallen against her neck. He had an urge to swipe those strands away from her tanned skin. Instead, he gripped the phone as he met her gaze.

"Thanks for calling. I'll be in touch."

He disconnected and went about making dinner without answering the question in Tara's eyes. They hadn't talked much about their personal lives since they had been separated. He knew she wasn't dating and he sure as hell had no interest in another woman. But they hadn't even discussed jobs or what was going on in general, other than to talk about Marley. Even then, they'd tended to text.

Yes, they should've been discussing more. The fact he wanted her back was reason enough for him to be more open, but he'd been giving her space... and he'd been terrified she'd reject him.

Living together was slowly changing how they communicated and Sam found that he wanted to get to know his wife all over again. If that meant they had to start from the very beginning, then he was willing to put in the time.

If he'd learned anything from therapy sessions, it was that repairing his relationships wouldn't be easy and it wouldn't be quick. He'd simply have to be patient and willing to fight for everything he wanted.

Sam met Tara's questioning gaze with a smile and turned to start dinner. He couldn't think of anyone else he'd take this much time and effort with, but Tara was worth the wait. She was worth absolutely everything.

Chapter Twelve

"Can we have a family game night?" Marley asked.

Tara stretched her legs out on the sofa and clutched the throw pillow on her lap. Family game night had been such a staple in their house when Sam lived with them before his addiction. Even during his addiction, when he had good days they still managed to make family night a priority.

Across the room, Sam met her gaze over Marley's head. He offered her the signature smile, the same one he had given her in the kitchen after the phone call with his boss.

That smile frightened her in ways she couldn't fully comprehend. He looked as if his entire world was perfectly okay, like there was hope for something she had no clue about.

Or was he keeping a secret? His phone calls weren't any of her business, but it had seemed that as soon as she'd come into the room he was in a hurry to hang up.

No. She was getting caught up in the fear she'd had in the past when he'd started sneaking away for his pills. That wasn't Sam now. She knew he was clean. Besides, she didn't have to know everyone he talked to. It wasn't like they were at the point of sharing everything, and he had a life without her.

Okay, that had been painful to admit to herself. But the truth often hurt.

"I didn't pack any games."

Tara pushed aside her swirling thoughts as she focused on Marley. Staring at Sam would only create another layer of worry and tingles…definitely not the best combo.

"I did." Sam jumped to his feet and turned from the living room. "I even packed your favorites, Marmaid."

Marley squealed and clapped her hands, causing Daisy to jump up and bark. Sam headed out and moments later returned with three board games. Tara couldn't help but be touched at his gesture; she'd had no idea he had packed those. Once again, he was thinking ahead and putting their needs first—no matter how minor.

"Which one are we starting with?" Sam asked as he laid the games on the coffee table.

Sam settled onto the floor beside Marley and Daisy. Tara watched as they figured out which game they would play, and then she slid from the sofa to the floor, resting against the cushions.

It wasn't long before they fell into the easy routine of playing games, with Sam cheating as he always did—though he was never subtle about it and always thought his tactics would go unnoticed or he could charm his way out of being called out.

"You can't land on red and pick up the blue card," Tara scolded. "You are not going to win, Sam. So you might as well give up."

Sam reached across the table for the blue card and waved it in the air. "I will never admit defeat."

Tara fully expected Marley to laugh as she always did but one glance at her daughter and Tara quickly realized something was wrong.

"What is it?" Tara asked as she scooted around the table. Her daughter's eyes were wide, staring straight ahead but not appearing to fully focus on one thing. "Marley?"

Sam quickly was at the other side of his daughter. "Honey?"

Marley continued to stare at the table, but she

wasn't blinking. The silence frightened Tara more than she wanted to admit. Marley reached up and rubbed her head, then closed her eyes.

"We haven't played a game in a long time," Marley whispered, then turned her attention to Tara. "Have we?"

Tara immediately glanced to Sam. His eyes were locked onto hers, and she knew the worry on her face mirrored what was on his.

"What makes you say that?" Sam asked.

Marley shrugged her shoulders and looked to the game. "I thought this would be fun, but when I see these games, I just feel…"

Tara settled her hand on her daughter's leg. "What?"

Marley's blue eyes once again came up to meet hers. "Sad."

Tara ignored the lump of guilt and the sting of tears.

"We don't have to play." Sam started gathering up the pieces and putting them in the box. "It's getting late anyway."

Marley leaned against Tara's chest and Tara wrapped her arms around her little girl. Every part of Tara wanted to open up and reveal the truth to Marley, but she had to trust the doctor's word and pray they were heading on the right path.

"Why don't I read you a story before bed?" Tara asked. "I brought your favorite mermaid book."

Marley nodded and stood. She threw her arms around Sam and said, "Sorry, Daddy."

Sam closed his eyes as he held their daughter tight. "Nothing to be sorry about, my sweet girl. I love you."

Tara blinked away the moisture that suddenly surged in her eyes. When Marley headed for the hall, Daisy obediently followed.

While Marley changed into her nightgown, Tara grabbed the book and settled on the edge of the bed. Daisy curled up right beneath Tara's feet. That dog could be a bit much at times, but she'd settled so easily in with the family and—

The family.

This is why she couldn't get involved emotionally with Sam again. They'd been living together for less than a week and already she was mentally referring to the three of them as a family.

"I'm really sorry, Mom." Marley climbed into bed, clutching her mermaid. "Are you upset?"

"I'm not upset."

"You're crying."

Children missed nothing. She willed her emotions to pause until she could get to the privacy of the bathroom.

"I'm sad that there are things you can't remember," Tara corrected her. "But I'm not upset with you at all. I'm sorry you didn't have good memories about the games."

"Why haven't we played them?" Marley asked, crawling under the covers and resting her head on her pillow.

Tara pulled in a deep breath and opted for as much of the truth as she could. "Your daddy has had to be away quite a bit over the last year and we haven't had the time."

Tara didn't want to get into the details. Instead, she cracked open Marley's favorite book and began to read the tale of the mermaid who fought to save her family from an evil octopus.

In a short time, Marley's eyes drifted shut and her breathing slowed. Tara closed the book as she watched her daughter sleeping peacefully, hating every part of this struggle while she and Sam knew the truth.

She wondered if this was how Sam had felt when he was hiding the truth from them so many months ago. Had he felt guilt while he'd been under the influence or had that not come until later? There was no doubt in her mind that he'd been consumed with guilt once he'd come back to his right mind.

Knowing Sam, he would beat himself up over this for the rest of his life. But she just couldn't let him in, no matter how well he seemed to be doing now and how much he worked for their family—there were just some injuries that could not be repaired.

Actually, she had repaired it as best she could

with a steel plate. There was no other way she could have moved on. The need to let him in grew more and more with each passing day, but in the long run, that could be detrimental to him.

She worried he'd use her as a crutch again and because she still loved him, she might let him and not even realize. Being a therapist and living out advice she'd give to others was so difficult. She truly believed people could and did change. She believed everyone had good inside of them. But… she was scared.

Tara sat the book on the bedside table, quietly tiptoed from her daughter's room and closed the door. She padded down the hall to the master suite but didn't see Sam.

The soft glow from the living room lamp filtered up through the hallway and spilled into the room. Silence had fallen over the house, unless she counted the heavy thump of her heart. The sound of crashing waves outside calmed her somewhat.

Here she and Sam were. Another night with so many unknowns, and she was exhausted. How long could she keep this up? The tension, the awkwardness, the fears. Between the lies to her daughter and her emotions for her husband, she didn't know how much more she could take. For now, though, she reminded herself that this was all temporary and it likely wouldn't be long before she and Sam went their separate ways once again.

With a weary sigh, Tara padded over to the bed and sank onto the edge. Her eyes burned with unshed tears and she dropped her head into her hands.

She couldn't break, not now. Maybe once Sam fell asleep she could sneak onto the balcony and take in the still of the night and the peaceful breeze combined with the gentle roll of the tide.

The soft snick of the bathroom door drew her attention. She glanced over her shoulder to see Sam standing there, steam billowing around him as he remained on display wearing only a towel and ink.

"I thought you would take longer," Sam stated as he walked to his suitcase. Again, he seemed to not have a care in the world and acted like all this was perfectly normal.

Even though Tara had seen his body multiple times, that didn't stop her from appreciating him now. As he shifted, she zeroed in on the one mystery that had been stirring up too many questions.

"New tattoo?" she asked before she could prevent herself from speaking.

Sam cast her a sideways glance and nodded. He offered no further explanation and Tara wanted to inch closer to see what he had.

He grabbed a pair of boxer briefs and slipped them on under the towel, letting the material drop to the floor.

Tara's breath caught in her throat. She wasn't

sure what was worse—the towel barely secured with a knot or the body-hugging boxers. Either way she was offered a delicious sight of his bare chest and firm thighs. The tattoos on his chest she was quite familiar with. They ran across his chest, across his shoulders and down to his biceps. Every tattoo he had told a story. Which made her wonder exactly why he'd gotten that new one. Because the more she studied it, the more she realized it was a door. Just that. An open door with some shading and other details she couldn't make out without getting too close.

"You look exhausted," Sam told her as he remained across the room.

Tara smoothed her hair away from her face and laughed. "I am exhausted. Thanks for pointing it out."

Sam shook his head. "That's not what I meant. I meant you look like you're ready to fall over, so why don't you get into bed?"

Tara's eyes went to the bed, then to her husband.

"We are both adults, Tara. I think we can be next to each other and sleep, don't you?"

No doubt she could lie in bed with her husband, but sleeping would be a whole different matter. Tara went to her own suitcase and pulled out her nightgown…the ugly old cotton one he'd always hated. No way had she thought of packing anything remotely sexy or revealing.

The hideous gown had a hole in the hem and the image of a hippo on the front. Sam had taken Marley Christmas shopping their first year together and that was what Marley had chosen. So, with Sam gone, Tara had chosen to wear this gown to pieces.

She clutched the material against her chest as she turned toward the bathroom to wash up and change. Sam never moved, but his eyes remained on her. The intensity of his gaze felt like a caress when he looked at her.

She wasn't naive and she was extremely familiar with every single one of those looks. He wanted her and he wasn't trying to hide it.

Tara stilled, wondering if he was going to say anything. He simply remained by the bed, his hands propped on his narrow hips, as if waiting for her to make a move.

At this point there was nothing more she wanted than to be comforted. To lose herself in a few moments of passion. But was that smart? What impact would intimacy have in the long run of this relationship? Because even though they were getting a divorce, they still had a relationship.

Pulling in a deep breath, Tara walked into the master bathroom and closed the door. She sat her nightgown on the edge of the vanity and rested her palms on the edge. Dropping her head, Tara let tears fill her eyes.

In moments, she was going to be curled up next to her husband. She wouldn't sleep. She'd lie there and analyze each and every one of her feelings. Come sunup she probably still wouldn't be any closer to figuring out how the hell to keep him at a good emotional distance.

Did this sleeping arrangement affect him at all? Did he have any emotions other than sexual desire? Because she had so many she couldn't even categorize them.

A sob escaped her before she could stop it. Tara lifted her hand to her mouth and squeezed her eyes shut. Tears slipped out one by one, dropping onto her hand. She needed to compose herself, to gather her thoughts, to pray for the willpower to face that bed and Sam.

The door opened then shut. Strong arms enveloped her. She found herself resting against Sam's strong, bare chest. She didn't fight the comfort. If he wanted to console her, she was going to let him because right now she needed someone, and honestly, this man knew her better than anyone.

With his arms crossed over her chest, Sam rested his cheek against the top of her head. Tara risked opening her eyes and glancing at the reflection in the mirror. She thought for sure she would meet his gaze, but his eyes were shut as he held her, with worry lines etched across his forehead and between his brows.

Maybe he was more affected by all of this than she'd originally thought.

Tara reached up and rested her hands on his forearms. Maybe, for this moment, they needed to console each other instead of fighting the emotions they were both concealing.

"I don't want you to worry about me," Tara whispered.

"I've never stopped." Sam's hold tightened as he murmured against her ear. "You're my world."

Oh, those words. Tara wanted to crawl inside some fantasy world and hold tight. Forgetting all of this nightmare, rewinding to two years ago would be ideal. But she'd never run from anything in her life. She'd always faced tragedy head-on, from starting the support group with her friends in order to deal with grief of her past to pushing Sam away when he'd needed more help.

But she'd been strong for so long. Seeking comfort right now wouldn't hurt anything…would it?

Sam kissed her head and Tara closed her eyes. "Don't be nice right now. In fact, we'd both be better off if you left me alone."

"You've been alone too long, Tara."

He smoothed the hair from the side of her face and rested his cheek against hers. Now he did meet her reflection in the mirror and she couldn't look away. There was raw desire mixed with compassion on his face as he stared at her. He hadn't looked at her in such a way in…too damn long.

Tara felt her grip on the situation slip. Was she even trying to hold on at this point?

She glanced at the closed door. What if, for just this moment, she left everything, her worries and fears, on the other side of that door? What if she took comfort from her husband? She was human and she wanted to feel something other than vulnerable. She wanted to feel in control of something, damn it.

"Sam."

She shifted to turn in his arms. Her butt hit the edge of the vanity and his arms came down, caging her against him. That bare chest was but a breath away.

For a brief moment, she hesitated, but Tara was done denying herself, denying *them.* Her fingertips slid up his abs; the muscles beneath her touch tightened as he sucked in a breath. She glanced from her hands to his eyes, instantly seeing the fire he fought. The clenched jaw and thin lips were a testament to his self-control—and she was about to shatter it.

"Don't hold back," she murmured, her hands trailing over his shoulders.

Sam shook his head. "As much as I want this, I don't think—"

"Good. Don't think." Tara threaded her fingers through his hair and pulled his lips toward hers. "And don't give me time to think, either."

Chapter Thirteen

She covered his mouth with hers, and that's when something exploded inside him. He really should be putting up more of a fight, but he was done resisting both his needs and hers. Besides, Tara clearly knew what she wanted and thankfully she'd chosen him—at least for now.

And now was all he was going to focus on.

Sam's hands flew over her, ridding her of her cover-up and peeling off that one-piece suit. He took a moment to simply stare. Because no matter how much of a hurry he was in, he wanted to take a minute to admire the hell out of his sexy wife.

Her fingers curled inside the waistband of his

shorts, and with gentle movements she eased them over his hips until they fell. He kicked the unwanted garment aside as he fisted his hands in her hair and aligned his body against hers.

Joint moans filled the small space. Sam would almost have been content to continue kissing her and feeling her bare body pressed to his…almost.

Her arms circled his neck, and he lifted her up and sat her on the edge of the countertop. He rested his forehead against hers.

"Be sure," he commanded. "There's no regrets after this."

Her eyes met his as she tipped her head back. "No regrets, Sam. But no promises, either."

He hesitated, not wanting to cheapen what they were sharing now. What was the proper term for a one-night stand with his wife?

Her fingertips slid over the tattoo of the door. She deserved to know what that was, deserved to know the meaning. He was honestly shocked she hadn't figured it out. He'd chosen that particular spot so he'd see it each day he looked in the mirror. He needed that visual reminder.

Her eyes met his and he knew she wanted to ask about his new art, but now wasn't the time.

Sam gripped behind her knees and jerked them up over the outside of his thighs. She might not want promises, but that didn't mean he couldn't silently make them.

Without a word, Sam stepped close. His hands eased down the slopes of her slender shoulders and over the mounds of her breasts. She arched against his touch. He knew exactly where to touch her, exactly how to hold her to give her the ultimate pleasure. Their encounter the other night had only been a sampling.

Tara locked her ankles behind Sam and urged him forward. As much as he wanted to take his time, he hadn't been with her for over a year. His patience vanished.

He joined their bodies without hesitation and gripped her hips as she bowed back. He leaned over her, dropping kisses along her exposed neck. Her hips pumped against his and Sam had to flatten his palms on either side of her hips to hold his stability.

But damn he needed to touch her all over. He snaked one arm around her waist and brought her flush with his chest once more. Still completely joined, he lifted her off the counter and spun her around until her back was against the wall.

"Perfect," he muttered as he nuzzled the side of her neck where he knew she was sensitive.

He palmed her backside as her body started to quicken once more. She whispered his name over and over. He didn't know if he wanted to kiss her again or continue listening to his name coming out in pants. He took hold of her hands and laced their fingers together, holding them up on either side of her head.

Her knees tightened against him as her body trembled. Sam eased back, wanting to catch every single emotion as it overcame her, but his own pleasure consumed him so he covered her mouth.

Tara's short nails bit into his shoulders. He nipped at her lips as her body started slowing. Sam's trembling ceased, his breath coming in and out in a heavy rhythm that matched hers.

"I feel like I should say something here."

Sam smiled and let their arms fall as he rested his forehead in the crook of her neck. "You can compliment me on my mad skills or ask me to take you into the bedroom for a repeat. Either would work."

Thankfully, she laughed and smacked his shoulder. "Calm down there, stud. I think we both need a breather."

As much as he didn't want to let her go, she was right. That encounter had been so intense, and after all they'd been through, cuddling right now might not be the best idea.

Tara's legs untangled from his waist as he eased her to the floor. He smoothed a stray strand of hair that clung to her cheek.

"So, what now?" she asked, moving around him to grab her nightgown off the floor.

Sam watched as the horrendous gown slid over

her head and covered her lush body. As much as he'd hated that damn thing during their marriage, he couldn't suppress the smile now. He'd never suspected he would miss a hippo nightshirt.

"Eyes up here and not on my hippo." Tara crossed her arms over her chest. "I figured this thing was the perfect deterrent."

"Yeah, well, you thought wrong." He closed the distance between them and settled his hands on her hips. "But I'd never do anything you don't want or didn't ask for."

Her eyes flared wider as she inhaled sharply. As inviting as her aroused, shocked reaction was, he also knew when to back off.

Sam released her and headed to the bedroom. He grabbed another pair of boxer briefs from his bag and pulled them on as Tara stepped into the room.

"We're both sleeping in here." He left no room for argument or questions. "Which side do you want?"

Tara flicked off the bathroom light and rounded the bed. "Over here near the patio doors. I want to see that sunrise first thing."

He couldn't think of anything he'd rather do than catch a sunrise with her, but he kept the thought to himself. He pulled off the comforter and climbed between the crisp sheets. This entire moment was both surreal and awkward. He wanted to stay right here where everything seemed somewhat normal, but he also couldn't believe this was actually happening.

Sam reached over and clicked the light off, resting with his hands laced behind his head. Silence settled between them, the tension so thick he wasn't sure what to say at that point. After what had just happened between them, he knew they'd crossed a line they couldn't turn back from. Oh, she might have given the speech about this being "just for now" and "can't make promises," but that wasn't Tara. She wasn't a quickie type of girl. She had feelings; she had passion and love.

"Your silence is unnerving," she murmured into the dark.

"Do you want to discuss what happened in the bathroom? Because we're both replaying it in our heads."

Tara shifted and a moment later her head came to the crook of his arm. Stunned, Sam hesitated before he wrapped his arm around her. A warm, wet tear tickled his bare skin.

"Tara—"

"Just give me tonight. I'll be strong again tomorrow."

Her words gutted him and he tightened his hold as he turned his body into hers. "You don't have to be strong all the time. We need to lean on each other."

"I can't afford to," she whispered.

Who was she trying to protect? Marley? Herself? Him? Was she playing the martyr because she felt there was no other choice?

Sam refused to let her feel empty and alone ever again. He was back and back for good. He'd already gotten on his feet, was making decent money with a job he was proud of, and the next step was getting his family back.

Forever.

Something heavy landed on her. No, make that something heavy and wet.

Tara lifted one eye and peered over her shoulder. Daisy had wedged her way between Sam and her and was currently dripping slobber on Tara's shoulder.

"Daisy," Tara cried. "Off the bed."

Sam jumped up and raked a hand over his eyes and through his hair. "Come on, Daisy. Let's go outside."

So much for a beautiful sunrise that morning. She'd slept through it and had been awakened by a drooling beast who needed to go pee.

"Sorry, Mommy."

Marley stepped into the room and climbed up

on the bed, as well. "I didn't think you wanted me taking her out by myself."

"You're fine, sweetie," Sam stated as he pulled on a pair of running shorts and a tee. "I'll take Daisy to the bathroom. Then you and I will make your mom breakfast in bed."

Sam snapped his fingers and Daisy followed him from the room.

Marley squealed and clapped her hands. "I must be doing better, huh?"

Tara sat up and smoothed Marley's crazy bed head away from her face. "What do you mean?"

"You and Daddy are sleeping in the same bed instead of him watching over me," Marley explained. "I guess since I've remembered things, I'm doing better and you're not worried."

Not worried? Tara's list of worries was quickly growing and last night's weakness on her part only confused her more. She'd thought she could take comfort from Sam, and she had, but then everything had felt so good, so right. From making love to having him hold her and not try to convince her to take him back.

No, Sam wouldn't try to convince her with words. He was all actions and she was wearing down.

"You are doing better every single day." Tara wrapped her arms around her daughter and squeezed her tight. "The memories are coming slowly, but that's okay. You're healthy and no more headaches."

"I have an idea." Marley smiled. "What if we make Daddy breakfast? He always cooks. At least, I think he does."

It was true. When they all lived together, Sam had done the majority of the cooking with Marley as his trusty sidekick. Tara nodded and urged Marley to hop up.

"It's a great idea," Tara stated, following her daughter off the bed. "Let's see what's in there and we'll surprise him."

Tara had taken the time she needed last night. She had leaned on and used Sam for his strength and his support. But now she was back and needed to remain grounded and stay on course. She wasn't going to wait around for Sam to do things for her, even something as sweet and simple as breakfast in bed. But she was going to show her affection by spoiling him just a bit.

Just because she couldn't take him back didn't mean they couldn't work on a solid friendship. That would be best for all of them, actually. Because that was the best option at this point. Having Sam out of her life completely wasn't a possibility; she simply didn't think she could bear it again. But letting him into her life fully, back into her home, simply couldn't be.

Tara loved him so much, that letting him in could ultimately damage them both in the long run. As crazy as that sounded, she'd learned the hard way exactly what tough love was and now she had to live with her decision.

But, she wondered…what if.

Chapter Fourteen

After four days at the beach and a somewhat relaxing vacation, Sam knew returning to reality would be a harsh slap in the face. He would've been perfectly content to stay in that mansion on the ocean with his wife and daughter and Daisy.

But he was back and hitting it hard with a new design for the project he'd been assigned. Marley was visiting his mother and Tara had gone into the office to see some clients.

Sam sat in the office he'd always used when he lived in their home and stared at the blank paper before him. He was a little old-school in that he liked to do a rough sketch by hand before he took it digital.

Nothing was hitting him, though. All he could think of was how Tara had come apart in his arms and then cried on his shoulder moments later. He knew her tears hadn't been from regrets. Tara was afraid. She was worried about their daughter, but she was also terrified about her feelings for him. She didn't have to say a word; he knew her as well as he knew himself. She was afraid to fall for him again, but she was…and he was going to use that kernel of information to work on rebuilding their future.

He grabbed the pencil and hovered it over the blank page. His eyes went to the computer screen with the original draft pulled up. His mind had been working overtime to try to get everything perfect and not give the client another reason to change his mind.

After sketching and tossing wadded balls into the corner, Sam glanced at the time on the screen and realized nearly four hours had passed. His mother had said she would keep Marley all day because they were going to do some heavy retail therapy and get their nails done. Tara should be home from work soon, so he figured he should start dinner.

His cell vibrated on the desk and he spotted his boss's name. After nearly forty-five minutes on the phone with Bill, Sam was glad that he hadn't gotten too far in the design since there was yet another change. Minor this time, but still.

Sam disconnected the call after making plans to go into the office and meet with Bill and the client. So much for making dinner for Tara. He'd have to call his mom and ask her to keep Marley until Tara was home. He'd tried to keep his mother and Tara separated, but some things were unavoidable. He had a job to do.

The front door opened and closed; heels clicked down the hallway followed by a scurry of dog paws on the hardwood floor.

"Okay, girl, I see you," Tara cooed. "No, not on the shoes. Not on the new shoes. Damn it."

Sam laughed as he pocketed his phone and headed to the living room. Tara squatted to pet Daisy, getting a lick to the side of the face.

"I knew you loved her," Sam stated from the doorway.

Tara's eyes locked on his as she rose to her full height. That plum-colored skirt and matching jacket hugged her every curve and he wished like hell he didn't have to go to the office. He'd make use of their alone time together.

"I was going to have dinner ready, but I need to head out to the office."

Tara's brows drew in. "I thought you took time off."

"I did, but there's a project I'm working on and I need to meet with Bill and the client."

"Now?" Tara asked.

The hint of disapproval in her tone had him pausing. "I asked Mom to keep Marley for dinner, so you don't need to worry about that."

She stared another minute before shaking her head and bending to slip off her heels. "That's not what I was worried about," she muttered.

And then he knew. All this time he'd been working on gaining her trust and he might as well have been beating his head against a wall. Clearly, they hadn't made any progress at all.

"As much as I'd love to stay and discuss the fact you still don't believe me, I have to get to the office."

Sam stepped toward the door and grabbed his key from the hook.

"Sam, wait."

He turned, his shoulder brushing hers as his eyes landed on her. "No, you wait. I've done nothing in the past year to make you think I'm doing anything but working my ass off. As much as I'd love to stand here and continue to defend myself again, I have to go."

Without another word, he jerked the door open and turned to make sure Daisy didn't try to sneak out. He didn't slam the door, but that was simply because he'd already fixed the damn thing once after an argument and he didn't want to waste time doing it again.

Besides, slamming doors wouldn't help their situation. Sam was starting to wonder if anything would.

Tara had never been a fan of her mother-in-law, but Carol had always been good to Marley. She'd called and asked if Marley could spend the night with her and come home in the morning after breakfast. As much as Tara wanted her daughter with her, she was thankful for an evening where she could think through her feelings.

But having a few hours of peace and quiet wouldn't necessarily give her the answers she needed. She'd hurt Sam earlier and that was the last thing she'd wanted to do. She knew he'd worked hard, she knew he was evolving into a new man, but for a split second she'd been thrust into the past when he'd tell her he had to go out. She couldn't help it; she was human.

He used to disappear and for a time, she hadn't known why. Later she realized he was taking his pills and needing to escape so she didn't realize what he was up to, and then later he tried quitting but the addiction had been too strong and he'd started sneaking, lying.

He'd left believing she thought the worst and he'd been gone for hours. While she fully believed he was at work, she also worried something would set him back. The amnesia with Marley or the way she'd handled their encounter earlier—would either of those make him seek something to numb the pain?

She'd never believed in the past that he'd get addicted, so she truly had no idea what would keep him clean now. Did he have cravings? Did he struggle?

Questions she should ask instead of hiding behind her fear of the unknown.

She opened the screen door and let Daisy out to use the bathroom. Tara hadn't eaten for most of the day because her caseload had been heavy. Then she'd talked to Lucy on the phone about Kate's baby shower. So the little pack of pretzels she'd had at her desk had long since worn off.

She looked through the pantry to figure out what to make. She'd been spoiled when Sam lived here and she'd come home from work to a nice meal. Then, when he'd left, she'd cooked for herself and Marley, but that wasn't the same. The whole family feel had been gone and there was only so much mac 'n' cheese a girl could eat before she started noticing her waistline expanding.

Tara went to the fridge and found some steaks she'd picked up the other day. She wasn't sure when Sam would be home, but she could have a meal for him when he got here. A peace offering of sorts.

She grilled the steaks while Daisy let out some energy. Tara decided to set the table on the deck since it was so nice outside. The sun was slowly starting to descend, but that only added to the beauty of the evening.

She made up a nice salad and even threw some veggies on the grill, just like she knew Sam enjoyed. She owed him a major apology and hopefully this meal would help segue into her groveling.

Tara was stirring the sugar into some tea when the front door opened and closed. She tapped the spoon on the side of the glass pitcher and set the spoon in the sink. Sam's footsteps neared and she braced herself before she spun around.

He leaned against the doorjamb and simply stared across the room at her.

"I made dinner," she said with a smile. "Want to eat outside?"

For a moment, she wondered if he was going to even reply, but he finally offered a simple nod before pushing off the door frame and stepping into the kitchen.

Tara busied herself getting drinks and taking them out back. Sam disappeared into the office before he came out and took a seat in one of the patio chairs. Tara let Daisy inside so they could eat without a giant dog head right at table height.

"I hope you're hungry," she said as she settled adjacent to him. "I was so busy I didn't get to eat much and then I put on the biggest steaks and made a huge salad and then I figured you'd want some vegetables on the grill and—"

"Relax." Sam covered her hand with his. "Were you a nervous wreck the whole time I was gone?"

Tara sagged deeper into her chair. "Pretty much. Listen, Sam, I'm sorry. I didn't mean to hurt you or make you think I don't trust you. This is all so difficult and sometimes I get stuck in the past. I'm scared but there's no excuse for how I treated you."

Sam eased his hand away. "No excuse? You don't need to make an excuse for how you feel. Yes, it hurts to think you don't trust what I'm saying, but that's all on me for putting you in that position to begin with."

"Are we okay?" she asked.

Sam smiled, but there was a sadness in his eyes and she knew he was still upset over their encounter. "Yeah. We're good."

He didn't speak again as he dished up her salad and vegetables. There he went again, doing little things for her. That part of him had never changed and she'd be lying if she said she didn't enjoy that caring side of him.

"Has Mom not brought Marley home yet?" he asked as he cut up his steak.

"Oh, she called earlier and wanted Marley to spend the night. I hope that was okay."

Sam met her eyes. "Fine. I'm surprised you didn't mind."

Tara shrugged. "We may not see eye to eye on many things, but we both love Marley and I know Marley will have a good time. If anything happens, your mom will call."

Sam reached for his glass and sat there with his fingers curled around the drink. "You've changed."

Tara blinked. "Excuse me?"

"You've changed over the past year," he repeated. "You and my mother always dodged each other, and then when I started my downward spiral, you guys flat-out hated each other."

"Hate is a strong word," Tara replied. "We simply didn't agree on what was best for you."

Sam took a sip and then eased forward in his seat. "She never thought you should've kicked me out."

Tara slowly set her fork on the plate. "And what do you think? Now that we are past that point in time. Looking back, what would you have done had you been me?"

"Exactly the same thing."

Tara was stunned. She'd never expected him to agree with her, and he hadn't even hesitated. "You're serious."

Sam pushed his plate aside and kept his eyes locked onto hers. "I know you had to push me out.

I never would've gotten the help I needed had you not."

The invisible vise on her heart tightened. She had never heard him admit that before and all he did was confirm that she had been partly enabling him. Not because she wanted to, but because she'd thought he would get better on his own or with her help. She'd contacted some of her associates to reach out to Sam when she'd forced him out of their home. She couldn't just leave him with nothing, but making him leave was the only way she could think of to make him realize the severity of the situation.

"That's why you can't come back." She said the words before she could think not to. "I mean—"

"You think letting me in will…what? Make me turn to the pills?"

When he said the words out loud, it didn't sound as logical as it had inside her head, but damn it, she couldn't risk it.

"I think I'm scared and the last thing I want to do is risk your future over my selfishness."

Her last word came out broken and she realized she'd raised her voice and was on the verge of a breakdown. She'd never intended to tell him her true feelings. She'd never wanted him to know her real reason for not letting him back in.

But there it was. She'd laid the words right between them and now he knew her heart.

As if her emotions hovering in the air between them weren't enough, the combination of his heavy-lidded stare and the silence was simply too much to bear.

Tara scooted her chair back and started to pass, but Sam's arm snaked out and his hand curled around the bend in her elbow. She didn't look at him; in fact, when his thumb caressed along her bare skin, she shut her eyes to avoid revealing her emotions.

"You still love me," he murmured.

Tara's chest tightened. Of course she still loved him. That wasn't the problem. The problem was all the chaos that kept attacking that love, that relationship they'd built.

Sliding her arm from his touch, Tara went into the house and was immediately greeted by a very eager Daisy. She tried to get out, but Tara held her back. Sam stepped inside right after her and kept going so that she had to retreat. When he shut the door, he didn't do it gently.

"We broke one door already," she reminded him. "I don't want to fight with—"

Sam hauled her against him and covered her mouth with his. Tara beat her fists against his chest, but he held on tighter. He slid his hands up her spine, into her hair, and tipped her head as he arched over her. Tara's fists unclenched and she found herself gripping his shirt, then she was tugging at it.

Apparently, there was a fine line between frustration and passion… She wasn't going to take the time to analyze that line right now. Over the past week, she and Sam had obliterated any relationship line.

This is what they both understood, what they both needed…and Tara would worry about the ramifications later.

Chapter Fifteen

Sam walked Tara backward toward the hallway, but when she wasn't moving fast enough, he hooked an arm behind her knees and supported her with the other arm. Sweeping her up had been something he hadn't done in too long and he earned an adorable squeal of delight, just like always.

Yes, she'd hurt him earlier, but he knew she was sorry. Her mind had been reprogrammed and it would take time for her thoughts to shift back.

But right now he had his wife in his arms and there was nothing that was going to interfere with this moment. She'd made him dinner, she'd apologized, she cared for him so much more than she was verbally expressing.

He loved this woman. He was going to fight like hell to keep her, to prove to her that he was a man of worth. He was done thinking he wasn't good enough, because he'd worked damn hard to prove he was.

Sam kicked the door closed to the bedroom and stalked to the bed. The sun had started to set and the orange glow cast a beam of light directly into the room.

As he laid her on the bed, Sam took a moment to appreciate the woman displayed before him. So much had happened between them, yet here they were with another chance. But did she see it that way? Did she only want the intimacy or was she looking to build on this?

Sam reached behind his neck and gripped his shirt, yanking it off and tossing it aside. Tara raised up onto her elbows, her eyes roaming over his chest.

He made quick work of getting his clothes off, but when it came to her, he planned on taking his sweet time and enjoying every delicious moment of it.

Sam gripped the waistband of her shorts and jerked on the snap. Slowly he eased the shorts and her panties over her thighs and pulled them off. Tara sat on the edge of the bed as he stepped between her legs. Keeping his eyes locked onto hers, he unbuttoned her shirt…one button at a time until the material parted to reveal a pale yellow bra.

He grazed his fingertips along the swell of her breasts just over the top of the lace. Her body trembled beneath his touch. He reached around and, with an expert flick, had her bra released. She took over and threw it behind her, then reached up and wrapped her arms around his neck, pulling him onto the bed.

"I was going to take this a little slower." He laughed as he fell on top of her.

"We have all night for slow."

Sweet mercy, no other words could've made him more aroused or more hopeful. He was staying in her bed tonight and Marley wasn't even home. If that wasn't a testament to her true feelings, nothing else was.

Sam flattened his palms on the comforter on either side of her head as he joined their bodies. He looked directly into her eyes, wanting to see each and every emotion crossing her face. There was nothing sexier than seeing the passion and desire his wife displayed. There had been no other woman for him since he met her and there would never be another. She was absolutely it for him.

Tara wrapped herself all around him and nipped at his chin until he lined their lips up and gave her what she needed. He maneuvered their bodies and flipped over so she was in complete control. Even though he was a guy, he could fully appreciate a woman who knew what she wanted and went after it…especially since the "it" was him.

Sam circled her waist with his hands as she rested her palms on his chest. When she leaned down to kiss him, her hair curtained his face. Her hips jerked as he swallowed her moan. Tara's entire body tightened and trembled and he was helpless not to follow.

Her fingertips curled into his shoulders as she tore away from the kiss. Her cries filled the room.

Once the shudders stopped, Tara relaxed against him. Sam wrapped her in his arms and never wanted to let go. The sun had all but set now, yet the light from the living room filtered down the hall. At some point they'd have to get up and clean the mess from the patio and make sure Daisy hadn't eaten the kitchen, but for now, he was more than happy to deal with all the chaos later.

Tara rolled to her side and lay in the crook of his arm, her hand settled over his heart.

"I guess you forgive me for earlier," she joked.

Sam smiled. "I forgave you when you said it. I understand why you were concerned."

She lifted her head and rested it on her fist. "You're really a changed man, but the same…if that makes sense."

He knew exactly what she meant. He was the same, but so very different. He'd learned so much about himself over the past year. That you could get knocked down and be utterly defeated and still rise out of the ashes stronger than ever.

Sam trailed his fingertips up and down her spine. "I had to change. I had to be the man you and Marley need. I had to be a man I was proud of. I can look in the mirror and not be ashamed anymore."

"Sam." Her whispered breath tickled his chest. "I don't even know what to say."

"You don't need to say anything," he assured her. "I had to get better because I wanted to, not because anyone else wanted me to. And I knew if I didn't, then I'd never get my family back."

Her lids fluttered as she let out a sigh. He didn't want to hear what she had to say, so he pushed on.

"You don't have to reply," he added. "But you need to know where I stand. You need to know I'm not giving up on us."

Tara opened her eyes and granted him a soft smile. "Maybe I'm not ready to give up on us, either."

Sam didn't know that he could feel such relief, such elation—and too many other emotions to label—all at once. He wrapped his arms around Tara and rolled her onto her back.

"Say it again," he demanded. "Say you want to give us another chance."

She stared at him, her eyes misting as she framed his face with her hands. "I'm scared, Sam. What if—"

He nipped at her lips. “We’re not playing that game. The only thing that’s going to happen is we’re going to work on this family and be one unit again. Marley’s memories will return and we’ll be stronger than ever.”

“You make me want to believe it’s really going to happen.”

Sam took her lips, slowly coaxing her mouth open to let him in. Her fingers threaded through his hair; her legs shifted to let him settle between her thighs.

Sam lifted his head just enough to whisper, “Believe it. You deserve nothing less than everything I plan on giving.”

Tara had taken the biggest leap of her life the previous night. Waking with Sam next to her, knowing this wasn’t a farce anymore, was both scary and positively glorious. She hadn’t had such a burst of hope in so long; she actually felt optimistic about the future.

Sam had gone into the office that morning and Marley was on her way home. Things were slowly turning around and Tara planned on making sure from this moment on that her family came first. She and Sam were determined to make this work and as stubborn as they were, there was no way they would fail…she prayed.

The front door burst open and Marley came rushing in.

"Mom, look at my nails," she yelled.

Daisy took off toward the front door as Carol stepped inside. "Oh, my. This is one big dog."

Tara walked over to Daisy and grabbed her collar before the overly excited dog could slobber too much on Carol's shoes.

"She's a bit large," Tara agreed. "But that makes for the best cuddling. You know, when the drool is somewhat under control."

Marley bounced up and down, waving her hands. "Look, look. Rainbow colors."

Carol laughed. "She insisted."

"They're beautiful," Tara said as she admired the yellow, blue, pink and purple nails. "Why don't you take Daisy outside and let me talk with your grandma a minute."

"Okay." Marley slid her arms around Carol's waist and stood on tiptoe to kiss her cheek. "Love you. Thanks for letting me stay all night."

"I love you, sweet girl. You can stay anytime."

When Daisy and Marley were gone and the door had shut, Tara turned to face her mother-in-law. "Thank you for keeping her."

"Of course. She asked if she could stay all night and I've missed having some girl time."

Tara smoothed her sundress down and pulled in

a deep breath. "I know we've had our differences, but I want to start working on that."

Carol blinked and jerked back. "You're divorcing my son. A man who did everything for you and your daughter, and when he had a rough patch, you kicked him out."

"He needed to get help," Tara replied, keeping her tone light. "We want to work on our family again."

"Do you mean you need him in your life now that he's not sick?"

Tara rubbed her forehead. She should've let Sam handle this. She really should've, but she'd figured she'd extend the proverbial olive branch. Unfortunately, she'd been smacked in the face with it.

"I've always cared for Sam," Tara stated. "He needed help and he couldn't do that by staying here. I won't keep defending myself or my actions, but I wanted you to know that we were starting over."

"And what about when Marley remembers that you kicked her father out? What will you tell her?"

Tara shrugged. "The truth. That two people loved each other and fought hard to make their marriage work."

Carol pursed her lips and made some sound. Tara had no clue what that meant, but she couldn't risk extending this conversation any longer. Marley could rush back in and overhear, which was the last thing she wanted.

"Okay, well, thanks for bringing her home," Tara said as she moved to the door in her not-so-subtle way of getting Carol to leave. "I'll have Sam call you."

Carol didn't say another word as she took her opinions and left. No doubt she'd be dialing up Sam before she pulled out of the driveway, but that was Sam's issue to deal with. Tara had tried…which had been the story of their married life anyway. Obviously, Tara would never be good enough for Carol's baby boy, but whatever.

The door slammed a mere second before the scraping of dog paws scurried over the floor. Daisy came up the hallway, as eager as always, and Marley came running in behind her.

"Where's Daddy?" she asked.

Tara smoothed her hand over Marley's bed head. "He went into the office this morning. What do you say we get ready and surprise him with lunch?"

Marley's face lit up. "I'll go fix my hair and put on a pretty dress."

Up the stairs she flew with the massive dog on her heels. Tara simply laughed and headed up to get ready herself. She couldn't wait to surprise Sam. She truly felt like this was going to work. He'd been clean for nearly a year and still reported to his sponsor and was on the right track.

Tara went into the master bath to check her appearance and spotted a note in the basket with her makeup. Smiling like a schoolgirl with a crush, Tara reached for the slip of paper and unfolded it.

To a new beginning...

Catching her reflection in the mirror, Tara clutched the note to her heart. They were going to make it after all.

Chapter Sixteen

Sam had been gone much longer than he'd intended. His mother had called on some rant about his getting wrapped in Tara's web again…or some such lame analogy.

He'd been adamant that he and Tara were in love, that they were working on their marriage and that things would be better than ever. No matter how much he defended Tara, his mother had never thought the marriage was a good idea, so Sam was done for now.

After spending the majority of the day working on a surprise for Tara, he'd lost track of time and ended up doing more than he'd planned. But if everything panned out, he would have the ultimate gift for his wife and an amazing start to their new future.

As soon as he stepped in the door at home, Marley came running up to him. He'd barely braced himself before she launched herself into his arms. Daisy came running in, as well, and skidded to a stop…or tried to, but she ran into his legs.

"How's my girl?" Sam asked, kissing the top of Marley's head. "Did you have fun with Grandma?"

Marley nodded. "See my nails?" She flashed her hands in his face. "Where were you today? Mommy and I wanted to surprise you for lunch and you weren't in your office."

Sam stilled. No, he hadn't been in his office, which is what Tara had likely thought since he'd said he'd be working. But she couldn't know what he was doing or where he'd been.

Before he could answer, Tara came into the room but didn't meet his gaze. Great. Clearly, she wasn't happy.

"Daddy?"

He focused his attention on his daughter. "I had to step out. I hate that I missed you guys. We'll do lunch together tomorrow."

"I work tomorrow and I won't have time for a break," Tara stated as she started straightening up the living room.

She fluffed a pillow, she neatened the stack of magazines and she even lined up the remote on the arm of the chair. The place was spotless, but she was pissed and looking for a place to channel her energy.

"Since we missed lunch, can we make dinner together?" Marley asked him.

Sam sat her down and nodded. "Sure thing. Let me talk to your mom for a minute, okay?"

"I'll go get the pots and pans ready."

Marley and Daisy scurried off toward the kitchen. Once he was certain she was out of earshot, he turned to face Tara…who was now repositioning the photos along the mantel.

"I know you're angry, but would you stop and look at me?"

Her hands stilled on the photo of Marley from her first birthday. "I'm not angry."

He raked a hand through his hair. "You've practically got steam shooting out of your ears. Now, will you turn around?"

Tara released the frame and turned to face him. "What?"

"Do you want to talk?"

She let out a humorless laugh. "About the fact you lied to me again? About the fact your boss said he hadn't seen you all day and sounded utterly confused at the idea that I thought you should be there?"

"I can explain."

Tara shook her head. "You know what? Don't. I

thought we were getting somewhere. I really did, but the second I let you in, you lie to my face. I won't go through this again. You've been secretive lately and I'm just… I'm not doing this."

Sam propped his hands on his hips, battling over whether or not to tell her the truth. But he opted not to. Because, in the end, she would always have that niggle of doubt where he was concerned. No matter what he told her, she'd always question it.

"You shouldn't have to go through this again," he agreed. "Neither should I."

Marley stepped into the room, her head bobbing between them. "Are you two fighting again?"

"No, honey, we're—wait. What do you mean again?" Tara asked. "We haven't been fighting."

Marley's eyes welled up with tears. "Don't make Dad leave again. That's why I stayed at Grandma's so you two would talk and fall in love again."

Her words were slowly processing and Sam took a step closer. "Marley, do you have your memories?"

She bit her lower lip and rested her hand on Daisy's head. Daisy took an obedient seat beside Marley, like a big, goofy bodyguard.

"I want you to stay," she whispered.

Tara eased closer, as well. Sam risked glancing at her, but she only had eyes for Marley.

"Sweetheart," Tara said, crouching in front of her. "You need to tell us what you remember."

Marley sniffed. "I know Dad was sick and you said he needed to get better. Then he left and then you told me that even when two people love each other, sometimes they can't live with each other anymore. And then Dad got an apartment and he let me paint my room blue like the ocean."

She rattled on with more and more details of the past year and it was obvious she'd remembered everything.

"You say you stayed with Grandma so your mom and I could talk." Sam slid his finger beneath her chin and tipped her head up. "How long has your memory been back, Marley?"

"You'll be mad at me."

"Darling, we're not going to be mad," Tara insisted. "Please, we need to know."

Marley patted Daisy's head and hesitated. Sam wasn't sure she was going to answer until she finally muttered, "I remembered everything the night we were playing games at the beach."

So she'd known for several days. That would explain why she'd been trying to get them talking and alone. She wanted her parents together. If he hadn't been so concerned about her health, he'd have been impressed by her tactics. She was one smart five-year-old.

"I need to call the doctor." Tara stood and raked her hands through her hair. "This is wonderful news, Marley. I just wish you would've told us sooner."

Tears spilled down Marley's cheeks. "Please don't break up again."

Sam dropped to his knees and hugged his daughter. He pulled up every bit of self-control not to burst into tears himself. Just this morning he'd been so optimistic about their future, but now none of that mattered. He'd once again destroyed his family and having his daughter fall apart in his arms was all the proof he needed that he was toxic to her.

Tara immediately had jumped to the conclusion that he was lying, but that pain was nothing in comparison to seeing Marley's tears. The second-chance fairy tale might be over, but he was going to do everything in his power to slay his daughter's dragons.

The doctor assessed Marley and gave her the all clear. Tara had never been so relieved.

Unfortunately, she was reeling from all of the mayhem with Sam. He'd been there for the doctor's appointment, but there had been such a thick wall of separation between them since he came home earlier that she didn't even try to penetrate it.

She still had no clue where he'd been. All she knew was that he'd left telling her he was going to work, and when she and Marley had shown up, Tara had been shoved right back into the past. What had happened to all of his promises and the guy who swore he'd never hurt her again?

Lies and betrayal hurt.

Tara closed the door on Marley's room after tucking her daughter in for the night. The poor girl was terrified her father was going to leave and she'd wake up without him. Sam had promised her he wasn't leaving, but the "yet" had hovered in the air regardless.

As she crossed the hall to her bedroom, she rubbed her eyes and prepared herself for a confrontation. There was no way around it.

But when she stepped into the room, Sam was changing his clothes and the sight of his bare chest had her stilling in the doorway. Once again, her eyes were drawn to the mysterious dark ink.

"Why do you have a tattoo of a door on your chest?" she asked before she could think better of it.

Sam's mouth thinned, his nostrils flared. "I'd think you of all people would understand that."

Tara stepped closer, her eyes on the image of an open door leading to a hallway that appeared to be filled with…stars?

"I broke the door that last night I left," he stated, as if she could ever forget.

"You broke lots of things that night," she replied. "Why the door for a tattoo?"

"Look closer."

She took a step, then another, until she came

within inches of him. Staring at the artwork, she finally saw it…and her throat filled with a whole new host of emotions. Those weren't stars at all, but initials. Her initials and Marley's.

"Sam," she whispered, her eyes darting up to his.

"That door means more than the broken one." His eyes filled and she knew he wasn't far from breaking, either. "I needed a symbol to remind me what I could still have, what I could fight for. I needed something…damn it, I had to believe there was a future for us. That's all that got me through those rough days. I lied to myself and said I could have it all again."

She couldn't help herself. Tara reached up and traced her fingertip over the details. His taut skin stiffened beneath her touch. When he stepped away from her, Tara dropped her hand to her side.

"Where were you today?" she asked, shifting to keep her eyes on him.

Sam grabbed a T-shirt from one of the dresser drawers and pulled it over his head. Once he was covered, he turned and blinked several times, most likely to push the tears aside and put up that resilient persona once again.

"Working, like I said."

"Stop lying to me," she demanded. "If you met someone or needed to sneak around, I have to know what I'm dealing with again."

"Again." He repeated the word with mocking

laughter. "You immediately went to the worst time in our lives. Do you ever stop to think of all the memories leading up to that point? Did you truly believe I…what? That I went out for a fix today?"

Tara's heart beat so hard, so fast, she reached for the edge of the bedpost for added stability. Nerves swirled around in her stomach and guilt consumed her over the pain in Sam's voice.

"I don't know what I thought," she admitted softly. "I know you care for me, for us, but I don't know why you lied. Can you explain that?"

Sam let out a humorless laugh and shook his head. "Sure. I was working on something for you. You'd always talked about opening your own practice and I was meeting with a guy about a building he was selling. I was walking through and making a list of renovations and I was going to surprise you."

Tara gripped the post even tighter as another wave of guilt and frustration overwhelmed her. She'd jumped to conclusions when she should've given him the benefit of the doubt. She'd been a complete jerk. There was no way he would forgive her, and honestly, he shouldn't.

They both had their hang-ups and maybe they weren't meant to be together. Maybe there was just too much deep inside them to let them explore a new life. Perhaps all of those old feelings would continue to resurface and keep them in the past.

She absolutely hated that she counseled people for a living, yet she couldn't get her own life together. Maybe she needed to speak to someone again and assess her own demons, and try to wade through the chaos and war going on inside her.

"Saying I'm sorry is so… I don't know. It's not enough," she muttered, feeling like an absolute fool. "But I am sorry, Sam. I'm so sorry I hurt you."

Sam stood there, hands at his sides, all serious and sad, and she wanted nothing more than to cross the room and touch him. She wanted to rewind and take back her allegations, to remove all doubts from her mind, to believe that he was the man she knew him to be. But she couldn't do any of that and their second chance was gone because of her.

"I'm sorry, too," he murmured as he turned toward the door. But he stopped short and, without turning around, added, "I would've given anything to have my family again."

Tara's heart clenched as he glanced one last time over his shoulder.

"But both of us need to be in the present for this to work and you can't give up the past." He turned toward the hallway and muttered, "I'm sleeping on the couch."

Chapter Seventeen

"What do you mean, you guys aren't together?" Lucy gasped as she folded the pale gray napkins for Kate's baby shower.

The yellow, white and gray theme was both elegant and practical, considering nobody knew the sex of the baby. But since Lucy and Kate both knew that she and Sam were getting along and wanting to work on things, Tara felt like an even bigger fool backtracking now. Like, *yes, we're getting back together. Oh, wait, never mind.*

The uncertainty didn't sit well with her. She had had too much of that growing up, and the last thing she wanted was to live like that in her adult life and have her daughter subjected to an unstable lifestyle.

But Sam hadn't moved out. Marley had been clinging to him day and night. They needed to sit down as a family and talk, but Tara didn't have the heart right now.

Marley's memories had returned only days ago, so everyone was still tiptoeing around the important topics. Sam, however, hadn't slept in her bed and they actually hadn't spoken unless they'd had to.

"I tore his heart out," Tara stated as she laid a delicate yellow daisy on the folded napkin. "You know I texted that Marley and I were going to surprise him for lunch?"

Lucy nodded as she continued to another table. "That sounded like things were progressing nicely."

"Yeah, well, he wasn't there when we showed up and his boss acted like Sam never mentioned working that day."

Lucy stilled and turned. "What happened to him? That doesn't sound like Sam."

Another layer of guilt slid heavily over her heart. "You're right. The new Sam wouldn't ditch work, but my mind jumped back and I accused him—"

Lucy cringed, squeezing the cloth napkins to her chest. "Tell me you didn't."

"I did. It just came out, and I was scared and worried and… I messed everything up." Tara pulled out one of the white folding chairs and sank onto it. "He's right, though. I'm afraid that any time something like that happens, I'm going to let fear take over and I'll say something again that can't be undone."

Lucy set aside the stack of napkins and pulled out the chair next to Tara. "Listen," she said, reaching for Tara's hands. "You're human. You've both made mistakes, hurtful mistakes. But you both clearly love each other or this wouldn't hurt so much. If you didn't care with your whole hearts, then there would be no pain. Did he tell you where he was?"

Tara closed her eyes and nodded. "He was working on a surprise for me."

"Oh, honey."

"He was looking to buy a new building and was walking through with the owner and thinking of how to renovate it for the office I've always wanted."

Tara risked opening her eyes and looking at her friend. Of course, it didn't come as a shock when she saw sympathy staring at her.

"I don't even know if I can fix this, but Marley's memory is back and she's afraid—"

"That he's leaving for good now?"

Tara blew out a sigh and nodded. She had texted both of her friends after the all clear from the doctor regarding Marley's health. Everyone had been so relieved, but at the same time, that meant playing house was over and they were all back to reality. Too bad she'd fallen in love all over again with her husband.

"He hasn't left the house because we don't know how to do that to her again." Tara pulled her hands from Lucy's and pushed her hair behind her ears. "But the tension is so high, I don't know what to do."

"Maybe talk to him? Why don't you let Marley come over for a bit after the baby shower?" Lucy suggested. "We'd love to have her and you need the time alone."

Before Tara could reply, both of their cells chimed.

"Wonder who that is," Lucy muttered as she came to her feet.

They walked toward the area of the community center where they'd left their purses on the table near the rear exit.

Tara pulled her cell out and glanced at the screen. "Oh, mercy."

Lucy gasped as she read her message. "Kate is in labor?"

"It's too soon," Tara murmured and glanced at Lucy. "What should we do?"

Lucy looked around the decorated room and shrugged. "We carry on without her. She still needs the gifts that will be brought today and we can explain to everyone to keep her in their thoughts and prayers."

Tara replied to Gray's text and told him to call

as soon as they had news or if they needed anything at all.

"Well, that puts my problems on the back burner." Tara crossed to the final table they were setting up. "I really hope the baby is healthy. Five weeks is really early."

"I'm sure they will all be fine," Lucy assured her.

Tara pulled in a shaky breath. "They have to be."

Lucy placed the final folded napkin on the table. "Now," she said, turning to Tara. "We still have to push through our days, so after the shower, I'll take Marley home and she and Emma can play. Alright?"

In theory the day sounded perfect and the right opportunity for her to talk to Sam. But honestly, would he even listen to her? Had she damaged their new relationship beyond repair with her accusation?

"I'm not taking no for an answer," Lucy stated. "She can ride the horses. Noah would love having her help with them."

Tara smiled. "Marley would be upset if she thought I turned down an opportunity for her to ride."

"Then it's settled."

Tara took a deep breath. At least one thing was settled. Now she just had to face Sam and she only had a few hours to decide what to say to him to win him back forever.

* * *

Sam had dropped Marley off at the baby shower and then he'd gone in to the office. Even though he was technically still part-time, he needed to be doing something productive. He couldn't stay in Tara's house another minute. Being alone with his thoughts wasn't smart because then he'd start thinking about how close he'd been to having it all. How everything he'd thought he'd lost but fought for had been right in his grasp…but he'd lost it again.

He stayed out later than he'd planned and ended up at the office building he'd wanted to purchase for Tara. In all honesty, he still would. He loved that woman, even though she'd hurt him. He loved her fiercely and wanted to provide for her. He wanted her dreams to come true and he wanted to be the one who paved the way.

Even if they couldn't be together, what mattered was that she and Marley were safe, healthy and happy.

By the time he made it to the house it was well after nine. He should've called, but really…why? They were in a sense still keeping up the pretense even though Marley knew the truth. Sam didn't have the heart to tell her that even though they all loved one another, some relationships just weren't meant to be.

He couldn't say the words, because he was having a difficult time believing them himself. But love couldn't override the fact that Tara would always second-guess his actions and decisions. He'd come too far to live in the past. One thing he'd learned from his counselor was that it was okay to think of what happened, why he was such a different man now, but he couldn't be with people who pulled him back…no matter who they were.

The ache in his heart had only grown over the past week. Sleeping on the couch wasn't ideal and he truly didn't want to keep the charade up much longer. They were going to have to talk to each other and come up with a plan to talk to Marley.

Sam parked in the drive and headed toward the door. Daisy ran up and greeted him with a slobbery lick to his arm.

"Well, hello to you, too," he said, rubbing her head. "You ready to go inside?"

He followed her up onto the deck and opened the screen door, making sure she got in before he closed the door.

When Marley didn't come running toward him, he wondered where she was. Tara's car was in the drive, and Marley always wanted a hug when he came home.

Daisy ran into the living room, but Sam stopped short when he spotted a note with his name on it hanging on the refrigerator.

He recognized Tara's handwriting. Curious, he reached for the note and unfolded the paper.

It's my turn to leave a note. I'm sorry. I trust you. I love you. My feelings are that simple, yet that scary. I need you in my heart if you can find it in yours to forgive me.

Sam reread the note at least twice more, his heart swelling each time. In all the years they'd known each other, she'd never left him a note. He'd always been the one who would drop her random ones here and there, and the fact she'd kept them did prove she loved him…loved them.

She was reaching out to him, acknowledging her mistake. Hadn't he made a mistake, as well? Hadn't he destroyed their happiness? What right did he have to get angry when all of her actions stemmed from him?

Sam folded the letter and started through the house. As soon as he reached the base of the steps, she rounded the landing and stood at the top.

With one hand resting on the newel post, he held up the letter with his other hand. "My first love letter."

She offered a half smile and crossed her arms. "I thought it was time."

"How's Kate doing?"

"I haven't heard anything."

Gray had texted Sam and Noah earlier stating

he was worried that this was too soon for the baby. Considering Sam had no experience with pregnancies or labor, all he could do was offer support.

"Where's Marley?"

"She's staying at Lucy and Noah's tonight. I couldn't get her away from the stables."

"Maybe she needs a horse," Sam supplied. "I could build her a barn."

"You'd build anything for us, wouldn't you?"

Sam nodded and propped his scuffed boot on the bottom step. "Did you mean this?" he asked, still holding the paper.

"Every bit of it, but there's so much more and I don't know..." She shook her head and sank onto the top step. "I never wanted to hurt you. I'm scared."

Those last two words came out on a whisper and Sam started up the steps. Tara held out her hands.

"Wait," she ordered. "If you're not serious about us, if I've done too much damage, just don't come closer. I'm on the edge of losing it and I'm not sure how long I can keep holding it together."

Sam continued until he sank onto the step beside her. He wrapped his arm around her and pulled her into his side.

"Stop holding it together," he told her. "We're supposed to be here for each other, right? We're going to say things and do things that remind us of what happened. But we're going to be stronger and I'm not letting you take the blame for this. Not when it's all on me."

Tara sniffed and rested her hand on his thigh. "You didn't even make me beg for forgiveness or grovel."

Sam tipped her chin up and kissed her forehead, then the tip of her nose, then her lips. "We've had a year of hell. I'm not wasting time doing anything other than loving you."

Tara opened her mouth to his and he pulled her up and onto his lap. He cupped her chin and jaw with his hand, needing to feel the promise that only her kiss, her touch, could provide.

Tara's fingertips slid over his shoulder and feathered against the side of his neck. Gently easing back, he nipped at her lips one last time.

"What made you think to write a note?" he asked. "You've never done that before."

She smiled. "I want to be more like you. You're so giving and selfless. You're the man of my dreams and I want to do things that make you happy you're here."

Sam tightened his hold. "Being with you and Marley makes me happy. I don't need anything else."

"Should we go pick her up and let her know we're all staying a family?"

"No." Sam shifted her so she straddled his lap. "For tonight, it's just us."

Their next chapter began now and he was going to take full advantage of having his wife back for good.

Epilogue

"She is absolutely beautiful."

Tara stared at the bundle of joy. Gray and Kate had gotten the all clear to bring their precious baby girl home after a two-week stay at the hospital. Now, Fallon was nearly two months old and surrounded by everyone who already loved her.

Emma and Marley were doting all over the pretty little clothes and had already made her a member of their "girls only" club.

"How are you feeling?" Tara asked.

"Doing really well." Kate took a seat on the sofa next to Gray, who immediately wrapped his arm around her. "We're ready to be a family."

Tara understood that all too well. She and Sam

were starting fresh and loving every single minute of it. There was something so special about getting a second chance and they'd both agreed they were going to make the most of each day, each moment.

Holding this sweet girl in her arms, Tara smiled and had a hopeful outlook for the future.

"I don't want to overstay," she stated as she carefully rose from her chair and crossed to Kate. "I wanted to bring some food by and let Marley see you guys."

Noah, Lucy and Emma had just left. Sam had an important meeting he couldn't get out of, but he'd texted her an address and told her to meet him there as soon as she was done.

"I hope you like chicken and dumplings," Tara added. "Marley thought that was the best dish to bring."

"That happens to be my favorite," Gray stated as he shot Marley a wink.

"Can we bring Daisy next time we visit?" Marley asked, her tone full of hope—like that meeting would actually be a good idea.

"I'm pretty sure Daisy is a bit much for a newborn," Tara said. "Maybe when she gets older, she can visit and play with Daisy."

Marley nodded, her curls bouncing. "I can't wait."

"Don't rush time, little one." Tara patted Marley's head and glanced at the adorable new family.

"I need to go meet Sam, but if you guys need anything at all, please message me."

"We will." Kate cuddled her baby close to her chest and dropped a kiss on her forehead. "We're so lucky to have such great friends."

Tara ushered Marley toward the door and led her to the car.

"We're going to meet Daddy and then we'll go to dinner," Tara stated as she drove through downtown Stonerock toward the address Sam had given her. "You get to pick the place."

Marley clapped. "Really? Oh, I've really been wanting a steak. Can I get steak?"

Tara turned onto Cedar Street and glanced at the addresses on the buildings. Up ahead she saw Sam's truck parked in a side parking lot.

"I say we all get a steak," Tara replied as she pulled into the lot. "That sounds amazing."

"What are we doing here?" Marley asked.

"I don't know." Tara shut off the engine and grabbed her purse. "Daddy had to work today and asked us to meet him here. Let's go see if he's ready because now I'm hungry."

Tara got out of the car and waited for Marley to come around. She took her daughter's hand and headed toward the front of the building as Sam stepped out the front door.

"How was the visit?" he asked as he leaned into her and kissed her cheek.

"The baby has grown so much in two months," Tara said. "Marley and I are ready for dinner and she's chosen steak. What are we doing here?"

Sam's smile widened as he gestured toward the front door. "Go inside."

Tara released Marley's hand and tipped her head. "You're awfully mysterious."

She moved around him and pulled open the double doors. An empty space greeted her and she remembered.

Tara jerked her attention to Sam, who stood before her, smiling wide and holding Marley's hand.

"You didn't…"

Sam nodded. "I did. It's officially yours."

Tears burned her eyes and she rushed forward, throwing her arms around his neck. "I can't believe you did this," she cried.

His arm came around her back as he eased away to kiss her forehead. "I knew I was buying it. No matter how we ended up, this was going to be yours."

Oh, this man. He had a heart bigger than anyone she'd ever seen and he freely gifted every part of it to her. How did she get so blessed to be given this second chance? Not only a second chance with Sam, but at a new chapter in her career…and their personal life.

Tara pulled in a deep breath. "I have a little surprise of my own."

Marley jumped up and down. "Another dog?" she squealed.

Tara laughed. "No, I think we're good with Daisy."

She directed her attention back to Sam and smiled. His eyes widened.

"What?" he asked. "Are you… Tara?"

She slid a hand over her flat abdomen. "I am."

"What's going on?" Marley cried. "Am I finally getting my iguana?"

Sam grabbed Tara again and whisked her around in a circle. As he set her on her feet, he showered her with kisses.

"Do you feel okay?" he asked, framing her face as he stared into her eyes. "Are you happy? Because I can't tell you how I'm feeling. I can't find the words."

Tara laughed, placing her hands on his chest. "I hope that's a good thing that you're speechless. But, to answer your question, I'm feeling fine. I'm not sick or overly tired. Completely different from when I was with Marley."

"Mom, what's going on?"

Tara flashed a grin toward her daughter as she bent to get eye level. "You may not be getting an iguana, but how about a baby brother or sister?"

Marley's jaw dropped and for a moment Tara didn't know if she was going to say anything. Finally, she pumped her fist in the air.

"Yes," she shouted. "I'll take a brother and I want to name him George."

Sam laughed and settled his hand on Tara's shoulder. "We can't order up what you want," he told her. "But we'll keep George as a possibility if the baby is a boy."

"How soon will we get the baby?" Marley asked.

Tara stood and leaned into her husband's side. "Not until spring, so we have a while. But we'll need to get a room ready for the baby. Can you help me with that?"

Marley gave an enthusiastic nod. "I've changed my mind. I want a girl so she can join our girls' club with me, Emma and Fallon."

"Well, we'll have to wait and see," Tara assured her. "But no matter what, I know you're going to be the best big sister ever."

Marley tipped her head and grinned. "Will you at least think about the iguana?"

Before Tara could reply, Sam chimed in. "We'll think about it."

Marley squealed again and started running in circles around the empty space. Her screams echoed in Tara's ears, but it was the most precious noise. A happy, healthy girl and a life with the only man she'd ever loved.

She shifted against him and wrapped her arms around his neck. "You know I'm not living with a reptile, right?"

Sam shrugged. "Maybe you'll change your mind. You let me back in."

Tara nipped at his lips. "That reminds me. You need to shred those papers you never signed."

"Babe, I destroyed those long ago. I could never give you up."

Tara's heart swelled. She truly had it all now. Sam was back in her life, Marley had been healed and they were growing their family.

"You knew me better than I knew myself."

Sam kissed her once more. "I knew us. You're my life, Tara. You and these kids of ours will always be my life."

Kids. She loved that word and couldn't wait to start their fresh lives together.

* * * * *

COMING NEXT MONTH FROM

HARLEQUIN®

SPECIAL EDITION

Available June 18, 2019

#2701 HER FAVORITE MAVERICK

Montana Mavericks: Six Brides for Six Brothers • by Christine Rimmer

Logan Crawford might just be the perfect man. A girl would have to be a fool to turn him down. Or a coward. Sarah Turner thinks she might be both. But the single mom has no time for love. Logan, however, is determined to steal her heart!

#2702 A PROMISE FOR THE TWINS

The Wyoming Multiples • by Melissa Senate

Former soldier Nick Garroway is in Wedlock Creek to fulfill a promise made to a fallen soldier: check in on the woman the man had left pregnant with twins. Brooke Timber is in need of a nanny, so what else can Nick do but fill in? She's also planning his father's wedding, and all the family togetherness soon has Brooke and Nick rethinking if this promise is still temporary.

#2703 THE FAMILY HE DIDN'T EXPECT

The Stone Gap Inn • by Shirley Jump

Dylan Millwright's bittersweet homecoming gets a whole lot sweeter when he meets Abby Cooper. But this mother of two is all about "the ties that bind," and Dylan isn't looking for strings to keep him down. But do this bachelor's wandering ways conceal the secretly yearning heart of a family man?

#2704 THE DATING ARRANGEMENT

Something True • by Kerri Carpenter

Is the bride who fell on top of bar owner Jack Wright a sign from above? But event planner Emerson Dewitt isn't actually a bride—much to her mother's perpetual disappointment. Until Jack proposes an arrangement. He'll pose as Emerson's boyfriend in exchange for her help relaunching his business. It's a perfect partnership. Until all that fake dating turns into very real feelings...

#2705 A FATHER FOR HER CHILD

Sutter Creek, Montana • by Laurel Greer

Widow Cadence Grigg is slowly putting her life back together—and raising her infant son. By her side is her late husband's best friend, Zach Cardenas, who can't help his burgeoning feelings for Cadie and her baby boy. Though determined not to fall in love again, Cadie might find that Cupid has other plans for her happily-ever-after...

#2706 MORE THAN ONE NIGHT

Wildfire Ridge • by Heatherly Bell

A one-night stand so incredible, Jill Davis can't forget. Memories so delectable, they sustained Sam Hawker through his final tour. Three years later, Jill is unexpectedly face-to-face with her legendary marine lover. And it's clear their chemistry is like gas and a match. Except Sam is her newest employee. That means hands off, sister! Except maybe...just this once? Ooh-rah!

Former soldier Nick Garroway is in Wedlock Creek to fulfill a promise made to a fallen soldier: check in on the woman the man had left pregnant with twins. Brooke Timber is in need of a nanny, so what else can Nick do but fill in? She's planning his father's wedding, and all the family togetherness soon has Brooke and Nick rethinking if this promise is still temporary...

Read on for a sneak preview of
A Promise for the Twins,
the next great book in Melissa Senate's
The Wyoming Multiples miniseries.

If the Satler triplets were a definite, adding this client for July would mean she could take off the first couple weeks of August, which were always slow for Dream Weddings, and just be with her twins.

Which would mean needing Nick Garroway as her nanny—manny—until her regular nanny returned. Leanna could take some time off herself and start mid-August. Win-win for everyone.

A temporary manny. A necessary temporary manny.

"Well, I've consulted with myself," Brooke said as she put the phone on the table. "The job is yours. I'll only need help until August 1. Then I'll take some time off, and Leanna, my regular nanny, will be ready to come back to work for me."

He nodded. "Sounds good. Oh—and I know your ad called for hours of nine to one during the week, but I'll make you a deal. I'll be your around-the-clock nanny, as needed—for room and board."

She swallowed. "You mean live here?"

HSEEXP0619

"Temporarily. I'd rather not stay with my family. Besides, this way, you can work when you need to, not be boxed into someone else's hours."

Even a part-time nanny was very expensive—more than she could afford—but Brooke had always been grateful that necessity would make her limit her work so that she could spend real time with her babies. Now she'd have as-needed care for the twins without spending a penny.

Once again, she wondered where Nick Garroway had come from. He was like a miracle—and everything Brooke needed right now.

"I think I'm getting the better deal," she said. "But my grandmother always said not to look a gift horse in the mouth." Especially when that gift horse was clearly a workhorse.

"Good. You get what you need and I make good on that promise. Works for both of us."

She glanced at him. He might be gorgeous and sexy, and too capable with a diaper and a stack of dirty dishes, but he wasn't her fantasy in the flesh. He was here because he'd promised her babies' father he'd make sure she and the twins were all right. She had to stop thinking of him as a man—somehow, despite how attracted she was to him on a few different levels. He was her nanny, her *manny*.

But what was sexier than a man saying, "Take a break, I'll handle it. Take that call, I've got the kids. Go rest, I'll load the dishwasher and fold the laundry"?

Nothing was sexier. Which meant Brooke would have to be on guard 24/7.

Because her brain had caught up with her—the hot manny was moving into her house."

Don't miss

A Promise for the Twins *by Melissa Senate,*
available July 2019 wherever
Harlequin® Special Edition books and ebooks are sold.

www.Harlequin.com

HSEEXP0619